"In the weird and gorgeous tradition of Angela Carter and Kelly Link, Miriam Cohen has written a manifesto of postmodern womanhood. Her characters are hilariously neurotic, exquisitely self-diminishing, and yet grotesquely eloquent—perverse poets all, wandering the streets of New York or suffocating in the decorated living rooms of suburbia, trying their dire best to navigate life's labyrinths."
—**JOSHUA GAYLORD**, author of *When We Were Animals*

"*Adults and Other Children* reimagines the Bildungsroman, as childhood clashes with adulthood to create a beautiful and terrifying emotional story. By stretching the misconceptions of children so thin and so wide, Miriam Cohen creates a glittering, transparent fabric through which we can finally read more clearly the myths that invent us."
—**SABRINA ORAH MARK**, author of *Wild Milk*

"The girls and women who inhabit Miriam Cohen's dazzling short story debut are like voyagers into the foreign land of their lives and families. These characters invent, observe, dismantle, fabricate, dissect, turn inside-out and, as a result, we, her delighted readers, are led into a funhouse where daily life is shrunk, stretched and reimagined so that we are left breathless and gratefully altered. As if that were not enough, Cohen is wicked funny, crafting sentences so surprising and alive you'll gasp."
—**VICTORIA REDEL**, author of *Before Everything*

"Lies, misconceptions and self-deception are at the heart of Miriam Cohen's funny, scathing, and touching collection, *Adults and Other Children*."—**FOREWORD (starred review)**

ADULTS
AND
OTHER
CHILDREN

ADULTS
AND
OTHER
CHILDREN

Stories

MIRIAM COHEN

PUBLISHING

New York, NY

Ig Publishing
Box 2547
New York, NY 10163

www.igpub.com

ISBN: 978-1-63246-099-8 (paperback)

To my sisters, biological and otherwise

CONTENTS

NAUGHTY

All the shades from all the other houses are pulled shut, the eyelids of sleeping giants. Amelia's house is the only house still awake. Its shades are flung open. In every room, ceiling lights flicker and buzz like sheer-winged insects. Amelia's mother is outside. She sits on the wooden bench meant for guests, her arms crossed neatly in her lap, her chin upturned. Amelia sees she has her keys. She has not forgotten them.

Amelia can see her mother, but her mother cannot see Amelia.

Amelia opens the freezer door. Crystals of white ice chip off from the edges, to the floor. Foil pans of other people's food make a wavering tower. There is lasagna and meatloaf and, from the next-door boys who are her enemies, a chocolate moose. The chocolate moose is from their mother. There is a note attached that says, Congratulations!!!

Amelia is not to eat except at mealtime. This way her father will not say to her mother, What have you been feeding her? each time he returns from another country and cannot lift Amelia high into the air.

But she isn't going to eat the moose. She only wants to see him: the delicate chocolate antlers, brittle as leaf stems, the shaved curls that will serve as fur for his hoofs. When Amelia removes the bowl where the moose is kept, the tinfoil tower trembles a stumbling curtsey. She peels back the tinfoil covering, careful, at first, not to rip it, but then she rips it anyway. The tinfoil comes apart so easily.

She can smell the chocolate. It makes her collapse, just inside her own skin. It makes her want to say, Hello. She takes care not to look at the moose until all the foil is gone, until she can see him entirely. Soon all the foil is off, crumbled into stars at her feet. Amelia's spine is stiff with joy.

In the bowl there is only mud.

Someone has put a spell on the moose. Probably it was Oliver, the meanest and youngest of the next-door boys. She should have known.

Amelia skates her fingers over the mud's frozen crust. Because it smells so wonderful! Because there is more than one way to say, Hello. The ice is furry, and burns her fingertips. She does the best she can, using her nails, tiny and patient ice picks. She lifts her fingers to her lips. To her tongue.

After, she is thirsty. She unlatches the small door in the freezer. There are no live-in elves inside. This is where the ice cubes are kept. This ice is safe from spells. No one knocked on the door with the ice, their two arms outstretched. Amelia plucks an ice cube and slurps. Some of the slurp is her saliva, some is water, melted already from ice. Her mouth is so hot.

Mrs. Prym comes into the kitchen. Mrs. Prym is the imaginary nanny. She stands next to Amelia, clucking with her tongue. The lacy petticoat beneath her apron brushes against Amelia's leg, scratchy as fancy tights. The petticoat is nice and stiff, because it is held in place with another child's bones.

"What has your mother done this time?" Mrs. Prym says, gesturing toward outside.

Amelia shrugs. The ice is a tiny sliver against her cheek, a bitten-off nail.

Amelia's mother is still on the bench. She is uncrossing her arms and crossing them back, as if the baby is inside her still, her fists curled uncomfortably around the cradle bars of her ribs.

Mrs. Prym sighs loudly and fully, as if she is blowing out a cake full of birthday candles. "This is my day off, you know. I'm not supposed to be here at all. Mr. Prym is waiting for me at home."

Mrs. Prym does not have any children of her own. She does not like children. She and Mr. Prym are wildly, wildly in love. Amelia has never met Mr. Prym. And thank goodness! Mrs. Prym is difficult enough. She is a real handful.

The ice inside Amelia's mouth disappears. Amelia did not need to swallow to make it go away. It is just gone.

"Mr. Prym and I had a whole evening planned," Mrs. Prym is saying.

Amelia opens the freezer door again. The shredded cheese on the lasagna looks like it could be confetti. She sticks her finger through the cellophane. There is a small *pop* that is only a sound for her fingertip.

"Naughty pig," Mrs. Prym says, interrupting herself. She is gripping Amelia's arm all at once.

Amelia struggles but she can't free herself. Mrs. Prym slams the freezer door shut. There is a *whoosh* of cold air. Then nothing.

"Let me go," Amelia says. Mrs. Prym twists Amelia's arm tighter. Mrs. Prym is giving her an Indian burn. Skin flakes into the air. Amelia's arm may fall off. This is not totally impossible. She has seen it happen before with long balloons. The trick is to keep turning.

And then Mrs. Prym stops, abruptly, mid-twist.

"That was a warning," Mrs. Prym says. She wipes her hands in the folds of her apron. For a moment her hands disappear entirely into the creases, but then they are back.

Amelia rubs her arm. She feels as if she has swallowed a piece of ice whole, but she has not—that ice was melted into nothing.

Amelia leans over the crib to pet her baby sister. Well. She is not really her baby sister. Mrs. Prym says the baby is a changeling. Witches have the real baby. The witches live near the train tracks, in a house that looks like a pile of leaves. Amelia has seen this house, but she has never knocked on the door, because the house has always looked to her like leaves. This was before Mrs. Prym came to stay, of course. She has taught Amelia what to look for. Danger is all around.

There are also werewolves. The father of the next-door boys is a werewolf. Amelia watches him now as he leaves his house. He leaves without turning on any lights. His house is not like hers. It stays asleep at night. There are all those boys—they need their rest. They need to do their homework. This is what their mother yells to Amelia when the sky is dark and Amelia must resort to hopping inside the squares of invisible hopscotch boards.

Amelia stands on the radiator and watches the next-door werewolf cross his yard. He sits next to Amelia's mother on the bench. He sits very close to her.

Mrs. Prym glances up from her knitting. Her needles look like enormous cockroach antennae. "There isn't even a yarn string of space between them," she observes.

Of course not! He is a werewolf—he needs to press his face to Amelia's mother's neck, as he is doing now, to get to the blood. Amelia cannot see well enough, even standing on the radiator in the changeling's nursery, because they are outside and she is inside, and so she asks Mrs. Prym to describe what they are doing. Mrs. Prym has perfect vision, also X-ray. She can see through skin, all the way down to the bone. This is how she knows the sister is a changeling. She can see into her lopsided, jelly bean-sized, black magic heart.

Mrs. Prym squints. "They're holding hands," she reports. "And now she is running her fingers through his hair, and alongside his ear, and his chin, and—Oh my!"

"What?" Amelia says, leaning forward, trying to see.

But Mrs. Prym is involved in her knitting now. "Stop asking so many questions," she says. "You're on my last nerve." The needles click together. They do not frighten Amelia. The ends are not that sharp.

Amelia steps down from the radiator and sits for a while, watching Mrs. Prym knit. Mrs. Prym is making something special for Mr. Prym. It is almost their anniversary. They have been married for almost one hundred years.

The carpet scratches tiny waffles onto Amelia's thighs and the waffles make water rush into her mouth from the sides, and also from beneath. She is not to eat when it isn't mealtime.

Amelia stands and pokes her fingers between the bars of the crib. The changeling's skin is as soft as rose petals. Her hair is scraggly, like the silk that comes from a split-open husk of corn. Amelia is to be extra careful at the back of her head, where the hair wisps to nothing. The bones in her skull are much too soft.

"Did you and Mr. Prym ever want a baby when you were first married?"

Mrs. Prym puts down her knitting. "Absolutely not," she says. Her lizard-beard throat wobbles as she laughs and laughs. The laughter does not sound like a foghorn moving in from far away to so close it is a touch for Amelia's spine. It is not small silver bells that are heavy to hold.

"Once I was offered a child," Mrs. Prym says, after she is done with her laughing. "By a witch it was, in fact. The child was nice and slender. Not like you." She pinches a doughy ripple of skin at Amelia's waist and does not let go until pink marks begin to bloom.

"I could have entered her into contests. My wallet could've been stuffed as a Thanksgiving turkey. In the end, Mr. Prym and I talked and talked—we had some red wine, very expensive—and Mr. Prym convinced me. There isn't room in a healthy marriage for even one child. Not if the husband and wife are as in love with each other as Mr. Prym and I are."

"My parents have two children," Amelia says.

"Exactly," says Mrs. Prym.

"What are you doing, just standing there?" Amelia's father says. He's in the room now.

Mrs. Prym gathers her petticoat and leaves the room. Her footsteps sound like: hush, hush. She has no patience for parents.

"You're just going to watch her cry?" It doesn't sound like Amelia's father is screaming, but Amelia is not fooled. He is screaming under speaking, the way people breathe underwater.

Her father runs his fingers over the middle of his head where there isn't any hair. The next-door werewolf has hair all over his head, but that is only because he is a werewolf.

Amelia moves away from the changeling so her father can take her away.

"Next time, you come and get me when she's crying. Do you understand?" Her father looks out the window above her head. When she is older and taller, the place where he is looking will be her face. But she is still her age.

The changeling's face is dewy with tears that don't seem

entirely clean, like the beads on cellophane after it has been covering steamed broccoli. It is like someone invisible is hurting the changeling. Good. She's not a real baby anyway. The witches have the real baby.

Amelia's father lifts the changeling out of the crib. There is the red mark at the back of the changeling's neck. The mark is a bite from a type of bird called a stork. This is what the nurse at the hospital said. Amelia is not fooled. The mark is from a type of man called a werewolf.

Amelia's father makes a hammock with his arms and swings the changeling back and forth. Quickly, quickly. The changeling weighs almost nothing. Her father swings her so far in each direction. If he were to let go, the changeling would not need wings to fly. Her father does love the changeling. It does not matter to him who the real father is. Amelia doesn't need to worry about all that.

The window can be like a mirror at night. In the window Amelia's father and the changeling become large ghosts, hovering above Amelia's mother and the next-door werewolf. They look like they are all together, but Amelia is not fooled.

"You were in the freezer before," Amelia's father says. He is whispering. He is not telling a secret; the changeling has fallen asleep.

Amelia is not to eat except at mealtimes.

She digs her fingers into her sides, which are soft pockets. She twists. "I only ate ice," she says.

Amelia's father shakes his head. His eyes look smaller than they are supposed to look. The skin around them has them buried. "You're not telling the truth," he says.

She backs up against the crib. The bars hurt in a way that feels nice. They feel like bones. She doesn't have any bones. It's true. Touch me, she has told Oliver, long ago, when they were friends, before they were enemies. All over she is soft. See?

"Ice is water," Amelia says. If she is hungry she may drink water.

"When did you start lying like this?"

She does not mean to be a liar. She does not mean to be so hungry.

Amelia's father is still looking at the space on the window where Amelia will be when she is taller and older. The werewolf leans over Amelia's mother, dipping his face inside the saucers of her clavicle. Bone marrow is delicious. When it is mealtime, the bones go in the garbage. Amelia is not to eat the skin, or the parts of the meat that are dark. What is she, some kind of animal?

Amelia's father swallows. "You've got to do better," he says.

She watches the egg in his throat move up and down. The egg never goes away. It is there just in case.

Amelia's mother is throwing a dinner party!

"I'm still a person," she says.

The plates are porcelain. The forks and knives are made of silver. The reason they are black in creases is because Amelia's mother is not a maid. The napkins are cloth. The glasses are not made of glass, but crystal. Held to the ceiling light, they make rainbows.

These are the guests: the werewolf from next door, the next-door boys' mother, all the next-door boys, including Oliver. Amelia is to set eight places. Four for the children, four for the adults. The changeling doesn't need a place. Amelia's mother feeds her beneath her shirt. It is not magic. Mothers are a certain kind of animal called mammal.

Mrs. Prym supervises Amelia while she sets the table. Mrs. Prym does not lift a finger to help. Twice, she trips Amelia. Both times, a crystal glass shatters. Luckily, no one notices. Amelia's father is at the take-out place buying food—Amelia's mother is not a maid—and Amelia's mother is upstairs putting on her face. When her face is put on she will be as colorful as a male bird.

"Mr. Prym and I had quite a night last night," Mrs. Prym says. "He ripped my clothes right off me. We made that bed rock like a boat. He said he would kill me if he could. And I said, 'Oh Mr. Prym!' And he said, 'You cunt.' And I said, 'Call me that again!' and—well, the rest is private. It wouldn't be the worst thing if you didn't know."

Amelia steps carefully over the shattered crystal. On the highest shelf above the fridge there is a bag of crystal made from sugar, spun around small wooden sticks. That crystal is broken also, and so lovely.

"What will you do with the clothes he ripped off?"

"Well, what about that! I'll probably sew them right into a dress for you. It's so hard to find clothing that will fit you. It's taxing, Amelia. It's like tax season all the time with you."

Forks go on the left. They are not lonely, because they have the napkin. Amelia tucks them in. Most of the napkins do not flutter open. They are sleeping birds.

"Some clothing fits me," Amelia says, tugging at where the sleeves of her dress stop before her wrists do, etching bracelets into the skin.

"Oh, but you're lying," Mrs. Prym says. She raises her longest finger into the air and wags it like a tail. "Naughty."

Amelia nudges a tiny piece of crystal with her bare toe. It comes close to breaking the skin, but she does not push far enough. There is too much fat in the way. "You're a liar," she says.

Mrs. Prym raises her eyebrows. "Call me that again," she says.

Amelia doesn't want Mrs. Prym to be angry with her. When Mrs. Prym gets into one of her moods, she is absolutely impossible.

"Cunt," Amelia says. It is a nice word to say.

But Amelia is not Mr. Prym. She cannot make Mrs. Prym rock like a boat.

Mrs. Prym lifts her petticoats. Beneath, the children's bones glint like teeth in a dark mouth. They are sharp as swords, sharper, by far, than Mrs. Prym's knitting needles. The bones are yellow, like baby skin when at first there isn't enough oxygen. Amelia thinks for a moment that Mrs. Prym is showing off her legs, but of course she is not! Mrs. Prym has been married almost one hundred years.

Mrs. Prym snaps one of the bones off easily. The sound it makes reminds Amelia of when her father rolls his neck from side to side.

"The only thing children are good for is their bones." Mrs. Prym smiles, not like she is happy.

Relief pounds over Amelia like water from a shower turned suddenly all the way to hot or all the way to cold. "I don't have any bones," she says. A bag of bones she's not!

Mrs. Prym brandishes the bone, stepping closer. She steps on the crystal but it does not hurt her. She is wearing sturdy shoes, the soles as thick as stacked coasters. "You're just a naughty, fat, liar."

"It's true," Amelia says. Her voice is a whisper, but not because she is telling a secret, and not because the changeling is sleeping. "Ask my mother or my father or the werewolf." She ticks all the adults off on her fingers, starting with her thumb, ending with the one in the middle. She tries again, counting from the other side, but she ends up back there, in the place that isn't nice.

Mrs. Prym looks around the room. Her neck whips all around. "But Amelia," she says. "I don't see any of them here."

By the time Amelia's father is back home with the food, Mrs. Prym has shattered all the crystal. She has shattered some crystal directly over Amelia's head, trying to get to the bone. But Amelia doesn't have any. The shards are in her skin now, behind her eyelids, in her temples. They are very heavy.

It is much too late to cancel the dinner party. Amelia's father has already bought all the food. There are three white paper bags. One is torn and shredded at the side where a dot of grease has become a puddle. A loaf of pale French bread pokes through the opening. Amelia would like to rip this bread open, to feel the crisp crumbs scattering down her wrists, and in her hair, landing, some of them, in her mouth, the warmest snowflakes.

She is not to eat French bread. If she is hungry, she may drink water.

The changeling is strapped to Amelia's father's chest. Amelia's father acts like the changeling is a tie he happens to be wearing.

"Didn't you hear her?" he says to Amelia's mother.

Amelia's mother blinks. Her eyelashes scurry across her cheekbones.

"I was putting on my face," she says. Her chin crinkles like a fingerling potato. On a potato, those crinkles are also eyes. When the potatoes are cooked, the skin will stick there sometimes. It will not come off easily.

"I can't watch her every minute," Amelia's mother says.

"How could I watch her every minute?" Her tongue darts over her teeth. There is an amber smear on her front tooth.

"I'm not asking you to watch her every *minute*. I don't think it's too much to ask to make sure she's not destroying the entire house. I just think any normal person, any normal mother would be a little bit—just a little bit—concerned? curious? to hear glass breaking in the kitchen while your daughter's in there unsupervised. But, hell, what do I know. I'm just the husband, right?"

Amelia's mother touches her new face. There is skin colored powder on her skin, and blue over her eyes that is the wrong color and the wrong place for a bruise. It should be lower, and darker. But it is close enough. Amelia understands.

"Give me the baby," her mother says.

Amelia's father laughs under screaming. It is like his speaking under screaming, but scarier. "Oh, sure. To the mother of the year." He lifts the changeling just a little off his chest—the straps will not stretch any further.

Tendons climb her neck like ivy. She does not reach for the changeling.

"You want her?" His neck juts forward from the crisp wings of his dress shirt, slick and leathery as a turtle's. "Here."

He unstraps the changeling. The changeling wakes up, and at first, for a moment, does not cry. She looks around the room with ringed eyes, her frog arms and legs dangling and mostly still.

"Take your daughter. Keep her. I think I have my hands full enough."

Amelia can be a real handful.

"I will take her," Amelia's mother says. "Watch me. I will."

Amelia's father cannot throw the changeling—he doesn't

know the baby he is holding is not really a baby; witches have the real baby. And so he is careful. He hands over the changeling like she is made of the same fancy crystal Mrs. Prym has broken.

In Amelia's mother's arms, the changeling begins to scream. Her face is a red-purple, the color of certain cabbages. The changeling will not stop moving her arms and legs.

The guests have arrived.

"I brought a Shepherd's pie," the next-door mother says. She thrusts a metal bowl forward like it is a bouquet of flowers. "I still can't believe you're having us over so soon after the baby. I don't think I saw anyone for weeks after my boys. I couldn't deprive them of the breast! It wasn't me they were after—just the breast!"

She looks at Amelia's mother's chest, and then down at her own.

"There isn't a rule book, right?" she says. "They don't give you a rule book!"

"You didn't have to bring anything," Amelia's mother says. "I find cooking relaxing, actually."

Amelia pinches a bit of her mother's tights between her fingers. The tights twist easily as skin, but look shimmery and light, a bee's wing.

"You're not a maid," Amelia reminds her mother.

Amelia's mother says, "Will you stop that, please?" She reaches for her tights without lowering her head. Otherwise her breasts may fall out. The back of her hand is a quick flicker.

"Kids!" she says, not to Amelia.

"Tell me about it!" the next-door mother says.

Their smiles are as wide as cantaloupe rinds.

"Why don't you come in," Amelia's father says. He looks

only at the next-door boys. He doesn't look at the space above them, but directly into their eyes.

The boys shuffle inside. The older ones take off their shoes, but Oliver does not. He must remember this from when they were not enemies: no shoes in the house is a rule only in his house.

The werewolf is the last inside. He holds a wine bottle of blood by the neck. He must have collected the blood from Amelia's mother, drop by drop, night by night. The door closes softly behind him.

The table is set with plastic cups, the kind that can easily be peeled into flowers or octopuses, after the first slit is made. Everything else is still porcelain and silver and cloth.

"There isn't time for everything," the next-door mother says, picking up her cup, squeezing it gently, like a heart she does not want to die.

The children all sit at one end of the table, and the adults sit at the other. Amelia's mother sits next to her father, and across the table, the next-door mother sits next to the werewolf. Amelia is seated next to Oliver. The older next-door boys are side by side on his other side. It is like a more complicated game of matching: not chicken to chicken, and horse to horse, but chicken to chick, horse to pony, two things that are not the same, but that go together.

But Oliver and Amelia do not go together. If only the changeling were not a changeling. If only she were real. Then Amelia would sit next to the changeling, and the older boys would sit next to each other, and the husbands next to their wives, and Oliver would sit next to no one.

All around her, the forks are being ripped from their napkin beds, where Amelia had so carefully tucked them.

"There's no such thing as too much when it comes to Shepherd's pie," the werewolf says.

The next-door mother taps her fingers against her neck. "Shepherd's pie doesn't freeze very well."

"I know you put a spell on the moose," Amelia says to Oliver.

Oliver ignores her, running his fork down his porcelain plate like a small rake. The sound it makes is like a squealing pig or a crying changeling: awful. His brothers laugh. They turn their forks into rakes. Misty sprays of saliva shoot through the air.

"This is what happens when you have boys," the werewolf says. "Amelia, you would never do something as obnoxious as this."

Amelia understands that he is joking, but not the joke. The way he says "Amelia" makes it sound like "Amelia" is not her name.

"Well, she's usually too busy with the fork," Amelia's father says. "What?" he says. "What?"

No one has said anything.

"Let me help you with the food," the next-door mother says.

"The food!" Amelia's mother says. Nothing is burning or spoiling or getting cold. "Amelia, let's leave the men to it."

This means Amelia must get up and help serve.

In the kitchen, all the food has been removed from plastic containers and put instead into foil pans. Now, Amelia's mother moves the food once again, this time onto sparkling serving platters and trivets. She cuts a thin pinwheel of orange and places it on top of the chicken stuffed with another chicken. The orange sliver looks beautiful and wrong.

"Oh, usually I use a lemon, but I'm sure oranges work just as well," the next-door mother says.

Amelia's mother traces her thumb against the remaining

orange, over the bumpy peel, against its chapped-lip skin. She breaks it open. The sound is soft, Velcro coming undone.

"Amelia," she says. "Why don't you take the mousse out of the freezer?" To the next-door mother she says, "We haven't touched it yet."

Amelia has touched it. She remembers her ice pick fingernails, the way they burned, and how wonderful and thirsty the cursed moose had made her feel.

"I don't want to," she says.

"You don't want to?" Her mother smiles, not like she is happy. Her fingers pinch the orange until there is a clear release of juice, rushing out all at once.

Amelia says, "I just have to check something," turns, and flees.

Mrs. Prym is waiting for Amelia in the changeling's room. She sets aside her knitting.

"Well, well," she says.

Amelia can see that Mrs. Prym is almost done with her blanket. It is pale pink, with a white embroidered bunny. It does not look like the sort of blanket Mr. Prym would appreciate—he is far too old, and a boy.

"That blanket isn't for Mr. Prym," Amelia says.

Mrs. Prym nods. "It's for someone else."

Amelia feels as if she has swallowed a bone. She can breathe. But it is hard. "I thought you didn't like the changeling."

Mrs. Prym stands and approaches the crib. She runs her spiney knuckles up and down across the changeling's cheek. "I didn't," she says. "But Amelia"—in between her eyebrows a miniature ski slope appears—"compared to you."

"I thought you loved Mr. Prym."

"Men!" she says, the same way, earlier tonight, Amelia's mother said, Kids! Mrs. Prym picks up her knitting once more.

From downstairs Amelia can hear the clatter of silverware against porcelain, the soft tinkle of voices sometimes, when one of the next-door boys is speaking, rising louder so she can make out words. *Fine. Yeah. More.*

No one minds that she is not there. But isn't it mealtime?

"You know," Mrs. Prym says, "I've begun to wonder if you are even Amelia at all. I think you must be the changeling. Because they are all learning to love Karin. And they've had all this time with you."

The inside of Amelia's chest is a cup with the bottom taken out.

"But you said you could tell from the changeling's heart. Witches have the real baby."

"I'm cross-eyed. You know that." Mrs. Prym reaches beneath her petticoat—there are a few bones left. The bone she snaps off is toothpick-thin, and she uses it to clean the spaces between her teeth. She removes small clumps of algae. It wouldn't be the worst thing if Mrs. Prym's dirty mouth were washed out with some soap.

When she is done, Mrs. Prym tucks her lips into her mouth, tidily. She smiles this way, without her lips. "Perhaps the witches have you."

There is a knock on the door. Mrs. Prym gathers her petticoats—they are more difficult to gather now that so many bones are missing—and swoops out the window in a deflated creampuff of lace.

The knock is from Oliver. "They want you to come back," he says.

He kicks at the floor with the toe of his sneaker. He doesn't have a red mark at the back of his neck as the changeling—or the baby? Karin?—does, even though Oliver's father is also the werewolf. Oliver has fuzzy hair there, at the back of his neck.

Touch me. See? She can remember saying this to him.

Amelia puts her hand to her chest, palm flat. Beneath her skin she feels the light patter of her changeling heart. It feels real, but it is not. No wonder she does not have any bones, no wonder her body is so soft. Witches have made her. They have all been so easily fooled.

"I don't have to," she says. "They aren't my parents."

He digs deeper into the carpet with his toe but he is not strong enough to make a hole, not even one that is tiny. He is done with his message—he does not have to stay. He is not to stay. They are not to touch each other.

Oliver's hands flutter at his sides, a soundless stammer. His ears are slender slivers of peach. They buzz. When Amelia tasted the outer edges, to see, that once, this was what she found: the buzz.

"I hate them," he says, and does not turn to go.

They are not to touch each other, but she is not really Amelia.

The real Amelia lives near the train tracks in leaves that are really a house. No one knows about this house, and so no one will find her, and she will live there forever. The witches have many uses for her. They do not know what they would do without her!

And—oh, she makes their house sparkle. Her hands, palms outstretched, are marvelous pans for dust. Her body is a perfect broom. Between their knotted fists, the witches have no trouble grasping both her legs. Her hair swishes over the dirt floor until it is clean. Her eyelashes are thread for their buttons; her teeth are the pearls they twist between their knuckles on the days they are sad. They make dirty golden necklaces from her hair, and bathe in the bubbles that spring from her lips when, in her sleep, she breathes. And, when the witches are done using her for chores, one by one they mount her legs, and she is weightless, sheer as wing, delivering them across the flickering dark of a train-lit sky.

Amelia cups her hand to her mouth, to his ear. She tells him what she knows.

BAD WORDS

Yael's parents ask if she has any questions, and she does, but she suspects they aren't the right ones. She wants to know if she will have two toothbrushes now, or if she will bring the same one back and forth, its bristles wrapped in shredding tissue to keep from getting germy. Also, she is curious about when a divorce starts: if it happens all at once, or in stages, the way people are engaged for a while before they are married. She wants to ask if later on that night they will all have dinner together, or if the divorce has made that, today, impossible.

"Sweetpea," Yael's mother says.

It is a name she has never used before, and it comes out with the stiff precision of a too-literal translation. It occurs to Yael that she may not know her mother well enough.

"It's okay, you know, whatever you feel. It's perfectly valid," her mother says.

"Like she even knows what 'valid' means," says Yael's father. He has not said anything up until now, and his voice is low and hoarse. He has enough stubble at this point to make Yael itchy with even the idea of kissing him.

Yael's mother turns to her. "Do you know what that word means?"

Yael doesn't, but she lies and says she does.

"See?" Yael's mother says. She smiles at Yael as though together, they've done something that belongs just to them.

"What does it mean, then?" Yael's father is smiling too, but his smile is different. It's the one he wears when he plays tennis with her uncle and is winning. He scissors his knees back and forth.

Yael doesn't say anything. Sometimes, when she doesn't say anything, the question goes away.

"I can't believe you're doing this," Yael's mother says.

Yael folds her legs beneath her on the couch with her sneakers still on. The sneakers are pink and they have lights that used to flash when she walked but that, after weeks of flickering and fading, no longer work. There is dirt encrusted into the heart and star patterns on the bottoms of her sneakers, and the couch is white. Yael waits for her father to look up from his thumbs and say, like he's supposed to, "Feet." She readjusts her legs and holds them to her chest.

Instead, it's her mother who says, "Feet."

Yael waits for her father to agree. The couch is his favorite, because it used to be his grandparents', and even though it doesn't look old, it is. When they died, he inherited it, and the first thing he did when the movers brought it home was take off the plastic that made sitting in it squeaky. It is white and soft, and his couch. Now, the cushions are ruined with faint brown outlines of stars and hearts. With her knuckles, Yael smears the dirt around so the pictures blur, seeping into the tiny squares.

"So you'll just keep sitting there," Yael's mother says.

Yael's father breathes out through his nose. He reminds Yael of a stallion when he does this.

Yael's mother says, "You expect me to do everything," and then turns to Yael with a smile that's scarier than a frown.

She explains that, for the time being, they will all still live together, but the only difference will be that she will bunk with

Yael, on the foldaway bed beneath Yael's regular one that is supposed to be for sleepovers. Yael wants to ask how long "the time being" is, but it's another question, she knows, that is wrong.

At bedtime, her mother brings her nightgown, deodorant, Styrofoam wig head, and the book she is reading into Yael's room. Yael guesses the divorce has started now. Her mother removes her wig and places it its Styrofoam head. Her real hair always looks so disappointing when she takes off the wig. Everything about her is stranger, smaller, without it. The wig head has a disproportionately long neck. Also, her mother has stuck wig pins into the center of one of its eyes, and Yael half-expects it to bleed. She closes her eyes and feels the softness of her lid, the delicate, gel-like ball beneath.

Her father comes in to say good night to Yael while her mother is changing. She is in her underwear. *"Not right now,"* she says.

"Oh, come on," he says. "Nothing I haven't seen before."

"I told you not right now."

He sits down on Yael's bed. "I have a right to say goodnight to my daughter."

For a second, Yael thinks he is talking to her.

"Fine," says her mother. She takes off her underwear. She takes off her bra.

"I'm going to tell my daughter a story," Yael's father says.

Yael's mother walks across the room, naked. This is nothing for anyone to ever find out about. It's not nice. It's not modest. Good mothers, the ones who are pious and whose daughters' clothing always match, don't even take off the head-coverings in the house. Their hair is too private even for the walls. Their hair is for their husbands only. Also, good mothers have five, six kids, sometimes ten or eleven (though ten or eleven is a little weird, because then your hair might not always be washed—but really, Yael shouldn't speak, because she's not always that clean herself). The problem is there's something wrong with her mother's uterus, which is a word that's not nice to say in front of other people.

The bare skin of her mother's belly brushes the top of Yael's head as her mother reaches for her nightgown. The nightgown is red and made of silk. Yael has never seen it before.

"Once upon a time," her father says, and a part of Yael wants to interrupt, to tell him, no, she is too old for this, she's in second grade already, but another part of her wants to do what she does do, which is lean her head into the hollow of her father's neck. The itchiness of his stubble is a fair sacrifice to make for the vibrations of his voice humming pleasantly in her own throat.

"There was a fairy princess."

Yael smiles. The princess, she knows, cannot be anyone but her.

"And a dashing, chivalrous prince."

Yael does not know what "chivalrous" means, but she likes that her father thinks she does. She stores these new words next to each other: "valid," "chivalrous." Her mind is a shelf.

"Oh, and but this prince loved the princess. He loved her more than anyone loved her. But the princess, you see"—here her father stops and wags his finger in the air—"she was born without a soul. It was a defect she hid well, of course."

Yael's mother has changed into the red nightgown. It goes only to her thighs, and it's see-through enough for her nipples not to be a secret.

She says, "I'm just going to…" and leaves the room.

"Then what happened?" Yael says.

"What? Oh, why don't we wait for Mommy to come back? She wouldn't want to miss the end of the story. It's her favorite, you know."

They don't say anything after that. They just wait. When her mother comes back, it's with a bottle of lotion. She raises one leg onto the foldaway bed and squeezes a small circle of pink lotion onto the center of her palm. Then she rubs both her hands together and moves them slowly up her leg, beginning with her ankle, ending at the top of her thigh. When she's done, she switches legs.

"So the soulless princess," Yael's father continues, too loudly, "she seduced the handsome prince—"

"Chivalrous," Yael corrects him, savoring the sounds of this new word as she pushes it between her teeth and tongue like a candy bar's nougat center.

"Chivalrous," her father agrees. "The chivalrous prince fell head over heels for the soulless princess. Invited her right into his chariot. Married her with the finest rabbi of the land officiating. But it was all a clever ruse, wasn't it?"

Yael is not sure if he is asking her a question. She lifts her head from her father's neck.

"Nah, she was just taking him for a ride. She wanted his soul for herself, is all."

Yael's mother says, "Stop it."

"His soul, his checkbook."

Her mother closes the cap on the lotion. She laughs, but it sounds more like she is coughing. "His *checkbook*?"

Her father's back goes very straight. Even though he has not finished the story, he stands and kisses Yael on the forehead, the spot he uses to check for a fever. Her cheek is where she is supposed to be kissed goodnight. The door closes behind him.

The foldaway bed is still empty and neatly made, but Yael guesses her mother has forgotten about it, because she crawls into Yael's bed with her, her legs slippery-smooth. Yael looks at her digital watch and sees that it is midnight, and the world is not magical the way she has always imagined midnight to be. It's just the same. Yael turns over in bed so her spine matches her mother's and, together, they are the two sides of a butterfly.

Yael knows she should be sad about the divorce, but all she feels is excited. For show and tell today, she will have something to tell. She is grateful that her parents are divorcing now, while she is still in second grade, because strictly speaking, show and tell should have ended in first grade; it's only by the grace of Mrs. Friedman that they have show and tell this year at all. Definitely, by third grade, it will be something babyish and outgrown and altogether boring. For now though, show and tell retains its appeal, though the prize from a cereal box no longer means anything to anyone. Show and tell, in second grade, is serious.

Last month, for example, Aliza broke her finger during recess, and instead of telling the teacher, she waited, and the finger, which was by then blown up and a different color and bent back too far, was her show and tell. She had to go to home after that. The next day, her finger was in a splint, a disappointment because a splint is not a cast and cannot easily be signed. Yael thinks her show and tell will be better than Aliza's because it's not gross, and because, unlike Aliza, she will not have to leave the room before she is done. She will tell the class everything, and they will listen, and she will be special and popular and tragic.

On the school bus, she tries hard to act like this is a regular day. She peels the green tape off the seat in front of her, revealing yellowish foam that reminds her of cheese curls. She sticks her finger into the foam. It's soft and disgusting. She picks off some foam and holds it in the web between her forefinger and thumb, looks to make sure no one is watching, then stuffs the foam into her mouth. Now she knows what bus tastes like.

Elisheva, who lives down the street, gets on the bus and sits down next to her. Elisheva does not eat cereal and milk in a bowl. Instead, every morning she comes on the bus with a plastic baggie of dry cereal. For lunch, she eats two slices of white bread that is a sandwich of nothing. She is very picky, like a queen. Yael eats cereal and milk in a bowl and a sandwich with peanut butter or cream cheese or tuna at lunch.

Yael holds her news inside her lungs like air before diving. And she knows, better than she has ever known anything before, that even though Elisheva has long hair, and the lights on her sneakers still work, and her sticker book is almost entirely full, Elisheva is not, after all, that great.

"Gross," Elisheva says, pointing to the seat. She untwists her baggie and begins to eat her cereal. Today it's cheerios. She eats each cheerio individually, sometimes sticking one on the tip of her tongue.

Yael sucks on the sides of her cheeks. "I have something cool for show and tell," she says.

Elisheva touches her cheerio-ed tongue to her nose. This is a trick Yael has tried, but cannot do. "What?"

"It's a surprise," Yael says.

Elisheva shrugs. Her hair is down to her tush, and when she sits, she arranges herself so that she is sitting on it. She tells people she has to sit on it. Yael watches her, and knows that she doesn't. She can, but she doesn't have to.

Aliza gets on the bus. Her finger is healed, and she doesn't wear the splint anymore. It's just a regular finger. Yael feels sorry for Aliza. She's glad a divorce isn't something that goes away.

The school bus pulls up in front of the elementary school. The doors open, like, Yael imagines, the chariot in her father's story. She feels like giving out her autograph.

After morning prayers and math, and current events, it's at last her turn for show and tell. Yael walks to the front of the room wearing what she hopes is a modest smile.

"She doesn't have anything, Mrs. Friedman, she doesn't have anything," says Shira, who has a custard-colored birthmark that takes up half her face. She bounces up and down in her chair like she has to pee.

"I can't hear you when your hand isn't raised," says Mrs. Friedman.

Though it is maybe the millionth time she has said this, Yael is always astounded by the willingness, on the part of her teacher, to lie, and so blatantly: there is no one, in the second grade, who could possibly be under the impression that, in the event of a teacher's inability to hear her student, she would say anything less than, What?

Shira raises her hand. Mrs. Friedman calls on her.

"She doesn't have anything."

Yael opens and closes her fists. "I do," she says. "It's just a 'tell', not a 'show.'"

"But it's show *and* tell, not show *or* tell," says Shira.

Yesterday, during recess, Yael told Shira that her birthmark was a slice of Munster cheese. She is dismayed at the thought that Shira would hold this against her. She had not even meant to be mean. Failing to share this revelation with Shira, the owner of the birthmark, would have been like finding a shape in the clouds and keeping it to herself, allowing everyone around her to see ordinariness when really, in the sky, was a dragon.

Yael thinks it is likely that she will cry, and after that, she will punch Shira, right in the stomach.

"Did you forget your show and tell today?" Mrs. Friedman says.

"It's a *tell*," Yael says.

"It's very important to be responsible and to remember when it is your day for show and tell. What if everyone forgot? What would happen then?"

Yael feels like her head is filled with bus-foam.

"I didn't forget," she says, and Mrs. Friedman begins to speak again, and her voice is firm and flat and getting louder, but Yael does not hear it. She does not hear it and she will not sit down.

"My parents are getting divorced," she says, and Mrs. Friedman stops speaking.

"Where did you hear that word?" she says.

"From my parents." Yael thinks her teacher is possibly the stupidest person she has ever met.

"Yael," Mrs. Friedman says, "it's very wrong to lie."

Yael is in trouble again. Only this time, it's actually not fair. Other times, when she has spoken out of turn, or pulled Elisheva's hair, or gone to the bathroom without asking, the note to the principal has felt inevitable. But the note Mrs. Friedman is writing now does not make sense. Yael wants to run across the room and rip it into confetti.

Two doors down, in the principal's office, Rabbi Klein smells of cloves. When Yael's father wears a suit, which is on Shabbos, he smells this way too. Rabbi Klein has a beard, which her father does not have. Some fathers do, and some fathers don't. It's better when they do. The reason he is calling her parents, Rabbi Klein explains, is because this is not the first note. It is not the second or the third or the fourth, but the fifth. He raises one hand in the air, almost like he is waiting for her to high-five him.

Yael may not go back to class while she waits for her parents; instead, she will sit on the bench in the secretary's office. She will not talk to anyone. If someone tries to talk to her, she is to tell them, politely, that she is in trouble and cannot speak right now. She will think about what she has done. What she has done is been disrespectful.

Yael likes the secretary. She gives Yael a butterscotch candy. Yael sucks on the butterscotch until it's a thin, translucent disc with tiny holes around the edges. The secretary answers the phone and types on the computer. Because there is no school nurse, when a teacher's aid brings in a kindergartener with a lopsided yarmulke and a scraped knee, the secretary is the one who helps him. First, she cuts a Band-Aid in half lengthwise. Then she crosses the two thin Band-Aid halves over each other. Holding the edges carefully, she gets up and places the sticky X on the little boy's knee, patting it firmly. "Good as new," she says, and then the boy gets a butterscotch. He takes the teacher's aid's hand and Yael watches them leave. She thinks he must have been pretending, for attention, because the kindergartner's knees bend easily as he skips.

Yael wishes she could ask for another butterscotch. If she could have just one more candy, she would be happy, completely. But even without the candy, she thinks this bench is somewhere she could live.

When her mother arrives, Yael is disappointed. Her bench days are over. She says, "Mommy," even though she is not allowed to speak, because when her mother is there, Rabbi Klein is less in charge. Her mother bends down to give her a quick kiss, and when she does, Yael realizes there is something off about her mother. It takes her a moment to see it exactly, and when she does, it seems impossible that it has taken her so long: her mother isn't wearing her wig. Yael checks her mother's left hand, but her wedding band is still there. She can't figure out what these two pieces of information mean together: only unmarried women don't cover their hair; only married women wear wedding bands.

Rabbi Klein calls them into his office. "This kind of repeated chutzpa," he says, shaking his head. "Behavior we just can't have."

Yael's mother crosses her legs and then folds her hands onto her lap. "My husband is sorry he couldn't be here."

Rabbi Klein nods and swats at the air, as if the apology is a bug he means to kill.

Yael folds her hands into her lap the way her mother has. She considers the phrase "my husband." Suddenly, she feels she has made a mistake, that she has somehow misunderstood, and her parents are not divorcing. It is like getting the chain call on a snow day, only to be called back, a moment later, with the news: there will be school.

"He couldn't get away from work," her mother continues, and Yael almost corrects her. She is absolutely sure that her father is not at work, because he has not been to work in two months. First he called his time at home "Being laid off." Now he calls it "Exploring other options." She knows it has been two months because her mother has put a star next to every day on the calendar her father has not been to work, and October and November are full of stars. She almost corrects her mother, but doesn't. Maybe her father just got a new job, and today is his first day, or else maybe he just got tired of being at home and went back to his old job.

Good fathers—the kinds with six or seven or eleven kids—
don't work. They have to study Torah all day because that's how
come the world gets to stay up. They're called learners. Fathers
who are less good, like Yael's father, are called earners because
they do work, but it's not actually the worst thing, because they
give money to the learners, and also they can give the school
all the money it asks for, which is called full tuition. And that's
also why, despite all the behavior notes Yael gets, her parents
sometimes get a plaque that says Parents of the Year.

This year, Yael guesses, there won't be a plaque.

"Of course," her mother says now, laughs. "Of course, *I* have
to work too."

Rabbi Klein wrinkles his forehead. Even when he stops
wrinkling, some wrinkles stay.

"Yael introduced a word to the class that may upset some
parents," he says. "Divorce," he says, glancing around the office.
"I don't know if that word could have come from a relative, or if
there's a TV somewhere…"

He looks at them like he knows they are liars and is waiting
for them to just say so already. But they don't have a TV. Yael
is almost absolutely sure of this. If they have one, she has never
seen it.

"We don't have any option at this point but suspension."
Rabbi Klein drops his head like he is sorry. The tip of his beard
makes a rustling sound against his tie.

"Well, then," her mother says. Her smile makes Yael's cheeks
hurt.

Yael's parents take her out for dinner that night, and it feels
like a celebration. The restaurant is *milchig*, so you can get pasta
with cheese, pizza, whatever's dairy. Meat is next door. The whole

block, basically, is kosher. There's also a bakery.

Yael's mother says she can order whatever she wants, so she orders chocolate-chip waffles. The waitress smiles at Yael's parents and tells Yael in a sing-song voice that it's dinnertime.

Yael's father takes out a five-dollar bill from his wallet. He reaches out as though to shake the waitress's hand, even though Yael knows he wouldn't ever really touch her: she is a woman who is not his wife.

Of course she doesn't shake his hand. "We really do stop serving breakfast at eleven."

Yael's father slaps the table and there is the five-dollar bill, wrinkled and small.

"Great. That's perfect," her mother says.

The waitress taps her pencil against her notepad, eraser side down.

"Can I get you something else? Or…"

Yael waits for the waitress to finish. *Or what?* she wants to know. Or the chef will make the waffles special for her? Or the waitress will offer to make the waffles herself?

"Do you want to order drinks, first?" the waitress says.

"I'll have a Diet Coke," Yael's mother says. "No, wait, Diet Sprite." She nods her head. "That one's caffeine-free, right?"

"It's a soda," Yael's father says.

The waitress asks if they need more time. She looks over her shoulder at the other tables, which are not filled with customers, because it's a Wednesday and it's nine-thirty at night, and people have to be at home.

"I'll take the Diet Sprite," Yael's mother says, and the waitress has no choice but to stay and take the rest of their drink orders.

Yael's father gets just water, for him. Yael orders a milkshake, which is supposed to be only for dessert.

The drinks come. The paper around her mother's straw is a swirl like a ribbon. Her father's just-water has a snowflake of dust floating in it. Then the rolls come, and the rolls are the best thing about this restaurant. Everyone knows that.

Yael's mother says, "I shouldn't."

"So don't," Yael's father says.

He raises his eyebrows at Yael. He can make it so his eyebrows go all the way up. She's supposed to laugh.

Yael sucks her milkshake through her straw until enough has gathered that her cheeks are full.

The waitress comes back. She taps her notebook with her pen. "Ready to order?"

Yael's chest is a fist. Chocolate-chip waffles are the only thing she wants.

Suddenly, she feels mean. "A cheeseburger," she says.

A cheeseburger is the most non-kosher food in the world. Eating a cheeseburger is the same thing as killing someone. She leans back in her chair and just waits. The sky will fall in.

The waitress squints at Yael. "I don't think..." she says, breaking off to smile at Yael's parents.

"What kind of cheese do you want?" her mother says. Her voice sounds like someone else's voice. "American, mozzarella, cheddar?"

"You're forgetting Swiss, feta, brie," her father says. He sways back and forth in his seat. Yael checks under the table, and, yes, his legs are scissors.

The waitress says she'll give them some more time.

But Yael would understand if she doesn't come back. The waitress is running out of some more time to give them. Soon, the restaurant will close, the waitress will go home, and Yael and her parents will have to leave, too, having eaten nothing, but

Yael now allowed, somehow, to eat cheeseburgers. Tomorrow, there will be no school for Yael because she has been suspended. But when the school bus does come for her, because one day the suspension will be over, she is not sure if the bus will be able to find her. She isn't sure she'll still be in the place she's supposed to be.

Her father gets up and leaves the table. It's just Yael and her mother. They don't have a ride home anymore. Yael's mother doesn't seem to mind. She drinks her Diet Sprite. Yael waits for her mother to remember that they are in public, that on her head, it's just her hair.

RECESS BRIDES

The new boy had the whitest skin. Veins streaked his temples like grass pressed into glue, splotches of giraffe skin freckles blooming up from a knit turtleneck. Jonah, Ms. Davidson explained to the class, could only attend school during the winter months, because of his condition. She lowered her voice on the word "condition," as if it were a secret only hers to tell. Jonah was also not allowed outside, but because it was important that Jonah feel welcome, since this was his first time ever in school, everyone had to spend one recess a week indoors with him. Jonah's parents had been generous enough to donate board games to the class. Ms. Davidson showed the class the laminated cards with Jonah's address printed on them for after-school play-dates. She paused before handing out the cards, tapping the pile twice on her desk.

Ms. Davidson picked Karin to stay inside with Jonah first, because Karin's last name was in the middle of the alphabet, and, Ms. Davidson said to the class, that was even more unfair than being at the end of the alphabet. She winked at Karin, as if she was giving her something everyone wanted. It made Karin feel like apologizing for not being better. She focused on the dried snot at the wooden edge of her desk, so it wouldn't seem like she wanted, especially, to stay inside with the boy allergic to the sun.

Lila, best friend to everyone, whispered across her desk that Karin's chance to be a recess bride had been today. *Oh well*, Lila mouthed. Karin rubbed her knuckle against her eyeball and tried not to think about the toilet-paper train she wouldn't tuck into the elastic of her uniform skirt. Ever since Ms. Davidson came to school wearing an engagement ring so huge some kids thought it was the kind that came in a plastic egg, or at the bottom of a cereal box, they found themselves drawn to the utility shed, where every recess became a wedding. The boys didn't play, so girls were called upon to act as grooms, best men, fathers-of-the-brides. There had been, in real life, a silver-scripted wedding invitation on each of their desks. The countdown was getting short.

Jonah didn't speak the entire morning. When Ms. Davidson asked him direct questions he shook his head, or nodded, but stayed silent. And every time he outright ignored her, instead of receiving an X next to his name on the behavior chart, Ms. Davidson she smiled at the new boy as if, in the slight shifts of his neck, he was telling her something she'd wanted very much to know. Karin worried she might not be able to keep from hating him.

During recess, Ms. Davidson left Karin and Jonah unmonitored in the classroom. She set the Monopoly box on her desk and pulled up two chairs. "So you'll have some room," she explained.

Karin kicked at the metal sides of Ms. Davidson's desk. The *boom* was low and echoing. "Do you want to play Monopoly?" she asked Jonah.

He chewed on the inside of his lower lip. His lips were bright red against his skin, and she wondered if being inside his body hurt. Jonah opened the Monopoly box and unfolded the board. He took a metal shoe.

"This is me," he said.

Karin took a horse.

She wanted recess to be over. She pictured her classmates outside, wondering who got to be the bride today instead of her, and who was stuck being the groom.

"Did you get invited to Ms. Davidson's wedding yet?" she said.

He crossed his arms and held his elbows. "I couldn't go anyway," he said.

"You can go to school," Karin pointed out.

"My mother wouldn't let me," he said. "Because the wedding's at night. So that's when I can go outside. When the sun's down." He reached into his pocket for a tube of Chap Stick, and ran it roughly over each lip. When he was done his lips glistened thickly, like glaze on a doughnut.

"I bet your mother would let," Karin said. "If you were going to a *wedding*."

Jonah shook his head. "My mother doesn't let me."

She didn't think Jonah was lying, but she also didn't fully believe him. It seemed impossible that his mother would have such unfair rules. She wondered if maybe his mother was just really a terrible person, and when he went outside in the sun the only risk he ran was of sneezing too much, or of breaking into hives. Karin couldn't imagine playing outside instead of dancing in a wedding hall that was real, with maybe Ms. Davidson telling her groom to hang on for one second please, and reaching for her, Karin, specifically and instead.

Karin had never been to a wedding before, but she'd seen pictures. She'd saved her parents' wedding album from one of the half-filled boxes piled in the basement, intended for charity or else the trash. Her mother acted surprised when she saw the wedding album, neatly centered on an extra pillow in Karin's bed. "I didn't know we still had that," she said, but later she said what she meant was she didn't mean for the album to end up in one of the basement boxes.

Jonah rolled the dice. He moved his shoe three squares. "My mother doesn't let me," he said, again.

"What happens if you go out in the sun?" she said.

This was a question she was absolutely not allowed to ask him: Ms. Davidson had warned the class of this before his arrival. Karin waited for something terrible to happen, for an X, maybe, to appear magically next to her name on the behavior chart, forcing her to be sent home again on the kindergarten bus, full with answers to give a mother who wouldn't ask.

"I'll die," he said. Karin looked behind her: on the behavior chart, next to her name, were two X's, same as before.

"You'll just drop dead?" she said. She raised both eyebrows because she didn't know how to raise only one.

"I would probably suffer first," he said.

Karin considered this. She traced her metal horse along her teeth, like braces, sort-of. Outside, girls harmonized the wedding march: *Here comes the bride*.

Jonah's mother picked him up after school, guiding him first into an oxygen mask and then a mini-van with tinted windows. His mother didn't look like him at all: from far away she even looked like Karin's mother. Their hair was sort of the same.

Jonah's mother kept a hand on Jonah's back until he was in the car. Then she quickly shut the door. She knocked on the window once before crossing over to the driver's seat. Karin waved at Jonah. He didn't wave back, maybe because he didn't see her, or maybe because being forced to spend recess inside together didn't make them friends.

She walked to the back of the school bus, where she was allowed to sit, even though everyone else was an older kid. They let her, but only because of her sister. Karin wasn't allowed to sit directly next to Amelia, but Amelia's compromise—because sometimes Karin did start crying—was to put a knapsack between them. The bus driver didn't really speak English, and for this everyone hated him. He made frequent threats about crashing the bus, but kids just yelled back, "*Good.*"

Karin tapped her chest three times, because that was the way to keep bad things from happening.

"Stop doing that," Amelia said. "You always do that."

"I'm not doing anything," Karin said. It was true: Right then, she wasn't doing anything.

Amelia tapped her own chest, but only twice. She didn't know the code, and if it had been up to her to save the bus from crashing, everyone but Karin would right now be dead.

"When you do that, you look like an idiot," Amelia said.

Karin strained to look out the window, but her sister's fox fur coat was blocking. The coat was actually their mother's, and it was much too long on Amelia, dragging over the floor so the bottom of the coat was matted and most often wet. Karin had a regular puffy ski jacket that made her look like a shiny snowman, and, at home, Amelia had one also, but she never wore it, and so Karin switched off wearing hers and Amelia's, so her sister's wouldn't forget how to be worn.

Karin's mother didn't care that Amelia had stolen her fox fur coat, even though, when she bought it, she'd said to Karin and Amelia, "This is it, girls," smiling so hard her shoulders met her ears, her pantyhose-shiny heels lifting out of her shoes. The fox fur coat cost fifteen hundred dollars, which, the saleswoman said, was a steal.

Karin leaned her cheek now against the coat, moving her head back and forth, so the fur swept her cheek like a soft-bristled brush. "Get off," Amelia said.

The school bus seats were ripped wide enough to hold small objects: someone's pudding-streaked plastic spoon, an old orange peel, a detached zipper. Karin added the metal horse. She hadn't known she was going to steal it until the exact last second, and then she did, stuffing it in her pocket as the class bounded in from recess, Lila with toilet paper hanging from the back of her skirt, unfairly, Karin noted: Lila had already been a bride four times, and some people, like her, had never been a bride even once.

Sometimes Karin's parents had date nights during the week, but because date nights were spontaneous, her parents didn't warn them in advance. So tonight there was a babysitter, and then her parents came home. Her father went to his room without speaking to any of them. He was still wearing his coat and gloves. Her mother shimmied out her coat, which was long and black, like a dress. It had begun to snow outside, and tiny ice crystals dotted the collar.

"He has a headache," Karin's mother said.

Karin wrapped herself around her mother's leg like a cat. "We love you," she said. "You're the best mother in the world."

Her mother patted Karin's shoulders without looking at her.

Karin thought that if she were a mother, she would feel so fortunate to have children who loved her, and she was afraid that when she did have children, they might not love her as much as she loved her mother.

"Should I take a plate to Daddy?" Amelia asked. She had already arranged two ketchup-zigzagged leftover hotdogs on a plate, and was heading toward the stairs.

Karin's mother threaded her fingers together.

Karin tapped her chest three times so Amelia would put down the plate and then sit at the table and tell a story about her day that would make everyone laugh.

Amelia held the plate to her chest. She walked toward the stairs slowly, holding the plate stiffly in front of her. The hotdogs quivered.

"She always has to be so good, doesn't she?" Karin's mother said. She sat at the table, and Karin sat next to her.

"Leaping to do the right thing. She doesn't know. Do you understand? *She does not know.*"

Karin made a doughnut with her arms inside her sweater. Her mother touched Karin's hands where they joined inside her sleeves. "He's just—he's a very small man."

Karin felt the way she did in school when Ms. Davidson acted like she'd said something smart or right, when she knew she really hadn't.

"There's a new boy in my class," she said. "He's allergic to the sun."

Her mother tapped her fingers over her lips. "It was different, of course, when you both were small," she said.

But her mother was mixed up: in the pictures and home videos, her mother was the same as she always was; in the *wedding album* pictures she was different. In the wedding album, her mother's hair was long, to the floor—almost really! And the camera didn't make it so her eyes were red, because these were pictures it was people's whole jobs to take.

Amelia came down the stairs still holding the plate of hotdogs. She put it down on the table. She sat in front of the plate, picking at the dead skin on her big toe.

Jonah wasn't in school the next day, or the next. After a few days, it was as if he'd never existed at all. It became the day before Ms. Davidson's wedding, and Karin was the only one who hadn't forgotten about him. She wondered if the sun from the other kids' faces had bled somehow onto his, and if this had made him die.

Karin asked Lila if she thought Jonah had died from being in school, and Lila said Jonah was a gross boy, and why did she care, anyway. She pointed to the boys on the other side of the classroom.

"Why don't you just be a boy, if you like them so much," she said.

She turned away from Karin and dug into her knapsack for a plastic bag of cookies, and offered a cookie to the girl in front of Karin and to the girl behind her.

Lila left the zipper open when she put the cookies back in her knapsack. When no one was looking, Karin reached into Lila's knapsack and ferried the cookies safely into her own desk.

During recess, the girls let Ms. Davidson be the bride so she could practice. Ms. Davidson acted more excited about the idea than anyone, and it made Karin sad for her. It was Karin's turn that day to be the groom. Lila said she had a surprise for everyone, and went to the coat closet, and lifted out a garment bag with only the hanger showing. She unzipped it with careful tugs at the zipper. And then she pulled out the dress with a flourish, like the magician who had visited the school at the beginning of the year. It was the most beautiful dress Karin had ever seen. It was pink, with ruffles at the collar and hem and sleeves. The buttons were shaped like flowers.

"It took forever to find," Lila said. "My mother took me

shopping every Sunday for a month, and then we found it, in the window, and they didn't have my size, but then the lady took it off the mannequin, and that one fit." She was breathless.

"You're going to upstage me," Ms. Davidson said, and laughed with her head back.

Karin felt as if she'd stumbled into the deep end of a pool when she'd meant for the intermediate. She hadn't known she needed a dress, and she hadn't asked her mother.

"What if we didn't get a dress?" she said, but quietly, and no one heard her.

She thought of her closet at home, but the only dresses she had were cast-offs from Amelia, which always looked wrong on her, as if they'd been donated by an anonymous charity, because, even though the clothes were from when Amelia was Karin's age, Karin was still a different person.

Karin's mother did take them shopping sometimes; it wasn't always hand-me-downs. Karin usually ended up with beautiful headbands that pinched the skin above her ears. "You'll wear this forever," her mother said of the headbands. And then they would shop for her, which was anyway more exciting. The last time they went shopping, her mother found a sequined evening gown that reached all the way to the bones on either side of her ankles. She wore it sometimes at home, but never when there were dishes in the sink.

Ms. Davidson smiled now at Karin from the other end of the utility shed. "Hi there, groom," she said, wiggling her fingers.

Karin felt suddenly furious. Inside her coat pockets, she clenched her fists. "I'm not really a boy," she said.

Ms. Davidson stood still for a moment. She tilted her neck.

"Of course you're not a boy."

Karin was sent home on the kindergarten bus once the missing cookies were discovered. Everyone in the class knew she stole, because she wasn't very good at it, and often confessed before anyone thought of accusing her. Ms. Davidson had leaned close to Karin, and for a moment, Karin wondered if her teacher was going to kiss her. "Karin, Karin," Ms. Davidson said.

Both her parents were home when the kindergarten bus dropped her off. They were sitting on the living room couch, her mother's hand on her father's shoulder. Karin dumped her knapsack down on the floor and they both turned around.

"Where's your sister?" Karin's mother said.

"I'm early," Karin said. "I was sent home." Her mother pressed the back of her hand to Karin's forehead. "You feel warm," she said.

Karin touched her cheek. She didn't feel warm. She felt cold still, from outside.

"I'm in trouble," Karin said.

"Is that so?" Her father smiled at her as if she'd told a joke. "Tell us about your troubles."

But she wasn't troubled. She was *in* trouble. Karin tapped her chest three times.

"How come you're home?" she said.

"Sometimes we have date night during the day," her father said.

"You don't want divorced parents, do you?" Karin's mother said. "How would you feel about a new little brother or sister? What would you rather? A brother, a sister, or a divorce?"

Karin's father started to laugh. "When you put it like that," he said. He put his hand on her mother's stomach. He raised one eyebrow.

Karin raised both eyebrows back. She liked being part of her parents' conversation, making a decision with them, the way, sometimes in school, everyone put their heads down on their desks and raised their hands in an anonymous vote.

"I vote for a sister," she said. "No, a brother." She hugged her shoulders.

"Now look what you've started," Karin's mother said to her father. She rested her head on his shoulder.

Karin didn't want to watch her parents. She tucked her hands into the waistband of her skirt, pretending a toilet-paper train.

"Cut that out," her father said. "She's touching herself," he said, not to anyone. He squinted at the floor.

Karin took her hand out of her skirt. She turned so her parents could only see her back and tapped herself six times on the chest, because she was sorry. There was something very wrong, she understood, with wanting to be a bride

Being a bride was like buying a fur coat or an evening gown: It made you look beautiful for a little while, and then it made you lock yourself in the bathroom and not come out until morning, when you pretended, over cereal, that nothing had happened. Karin wanted to warn Ms. Davidson, who laughed with her head back, and was beautiful already, even if that wasn't obvious at first. But she also felt like lying down on the floor and crying with her fists and legs, because she wanted, still, to be beautiful, to have a dress that was hers. She wanted a dress like Lila's that would upstage Ms. Davidson's.

"Mommy," Karin said. She tugged on her mother's free hand. Her mother swatted her away and it wasn't fair. She'd thought they both hated her father.

Karin went to her room and placed Ms. Davidson's wedding invitation next to her parents' wedding album. Outside it was snowing again. The sky was white. Karin wondered if Jonah could go out during the day if there wasn't sun. She wanted to know what had happened to him, and, also, what he did all day when he wasn't in school. She remembered the laminated card with his address, and arranged it next to the wedding album and the invitation. One, two, three.

She couldn't go to the wedding without a dress, but instead she could do something courageous. She could visit the boy allergic to the sun.

Karin left a note on Amelia's bed so she wouldn't worry. She copied down the number on the play date card, and also the address, just in case. "This is where I am," she wrote. The wedding album and invitation were lonely without the play-date card, so Karin copied down the address on another piece of paper for herself, and they all got to stay together.

Karin asked her mother if she could drive her over to her play-date. If her mother knew anything, she would know it was too early for a play-date—everyone was still supposed to be in school. But her mother didn't know anything.

"A play-date," her mother said. "It's so fun to be a kid."

Karin's mother called to her father that she'd be right back, and he called from the kitchen that she'd come back soon if she knew what was good for her. He was in love with her mother today, and this made him funny and loving and nice, even when he said things that would otherwise be mean.

Karin's mother swung the car keys between her fingers, and they chimed against each other like bells. Karin gave her mother the address, and her mother nodded. "This is close," she said.

In the car, her mother turned on music and sang along. She

had the most beautiful voice of anyone Karin had ever met, and her mother's singing made Karin feel like she was flying. Karin watched the trees and cars and houses move outside, and she imagined herself soaring above everything, and then her mother held a high note and Karin's skin felt tight, and she thought she might burst with how glorious she felt.

Karin recognized the numbers on the mailbox and unbuckled her seatbelt.

"Karin, honey?" her mother said. Her hands were tight over the steering wheel. "Do you think they look down on us, because they have a bigger house?"

Karin no longer felt glorious. She felt too hot in the car.

"It's not bigger," she said.

"Really?" her mother said.

Karin nodded. "Kisses," her mother said, and Karin swept her eyelashes against her mother's, once, twice, three times.

Jonah's mother opened the door.

"Well!" she said. She massaged the back of her neck with both hands.

Up close, she didn't look anything like Karin's mother. She was much less beautiful, and she didn't wear makeup at all.

"I came for a play-date," Karin said.

"We just didn't think school was the right choice, every day," Jonah's mother said.

"I was sent home on the kindergarten bus," Karin said.

Jonah's mother checked her watch. "But you're not sick, are you? Because if you are, I'm so sorry, but Jonah's resistance…"

Karin shook her head. "I got in trouble," she said. She put her hand to her forehead. "I'm not sick."

Jonah's mother's whole face changed into a smile, as if Karin were something valuable and rare. "It's cold out," she said, finally. "Come in."

The sofas were all covered in plastic, and all the windows had curtains. The shoes and coats must have been put away somewhere, because they weren't anywhere on the floor.

Jonah's mother called for him and he came downstairs. "You have a guest," his mother said. "Isn't that nice?" She squeezed Karin's shoulder.

Jonah knotted his hands together and looked at his mother.

"Why don't you go into the living room and pick out a board game to play?"

Jonah's mother seemed as nervous as if Karin were there to play with her.

She set out the Monopoly board she must have picked up from the classroom after Jonah stopped going to school, and also a game of Sorry! and Risk. Karin opened took out the Monopoly board and sifted through the pieces. The metal horse was gone. She felt a thrill at this, her power in this other house that wasn't hers.

Jonah spread the board over the floor. His hands were like porcelain doll hands. They could shatter just like that. She didn't realize she was touching his hand until it was too late, and then she thought there would be no point in pulling away, because it had already happened: She'd touched him. His skin felt just like skin.

She wasn't supposed to want to touch boys, and, in school, she didn't want to touch the boys in her class because of how mean they were. But she was glad to have touched this boy, because he wasn't a real boy.

"Your skin is so much darker," he said.

"At first I thought you were dead, but I don't think that

anymore," Karin said.

"Obviously," she added.

"What do you do in school?" Jonah said. He flinched, as if he thought she would absolutely not answer him, the way an adult might not.

Karin loved him now, because he didn't know, as a real boy would, that what she would play would not be what he would play; boys and girls couldn't play together anymore, some invisible boundary had been raised, and the only time they could cross it, ever, would be in the instance when they stood together and said they took each other, and owned each other now. After that, there would be separate bedrooms and dinners no one ate together, one or the other always so tired.

Karin told him about the recess brides, even though she knew this would no longer be true tomorrow in school. Tomorrow there would be a substitute, who wouldn't understand the game, and then, at night, there would be Ms. Davidson's wedding, and after that no one would ever be a bride again.

"We could play," she said. "Or we don't have to. I don't care."

He was staring at his hands, and it seemed like maybe he'd stopped listening to her. But then he looked up, his white, freckled neck thin and straight. "I'd play," he said. "You can be the bride."

EXPECTING

Ms. Perry wore platform shoes with open toes and the very sheerest of required pantyhose. Sometimes she'd even paint her toenails something crazy, like blue or orange. And she read the magazines they did—she could name all the different celebrities. Can you *believe* that wedding, this divorce, weren't those first five trips to rehab sufficient?

They wished Ms. Perry were *their* mother!

The students who loved her were a special kind of girl: glossy-haired glasses-wearers. Their cheeks were swabbed with body glitter sparkling of tiny moons and stars and hearts, maybe, but they were serious about taking notes. They had ambitions.

She told them, believe her, they didn't wish that.

Ms. Perry was so modest!

The bell rang—and they leapt! They flitted! Pleated skirts opened like umbrellas against rain. It was difficult to avoid seeing who still wore sturdy little girl underwear, and who'd graduated, startlingly, to low-rise bikini bottoms. Ms. Perry always saw more than she intended to see.

The highly relevant example: Amelia Miller, vomiting in the girls' bathroom. Ms. Perry had been in there to vomit herself—not after a night of boozing. After a night, that turned into a very early morning, of getting tipsier than she'd planned, or imagined she was. And on pear martinis, dusted with cinnamon, like pastries. But not, Ms. Perry saw now, exactly like pastries.

She'd been on a date that was clearly going to end up nowhere, not even in bed—he'd told her as much, basically—and she'd want to impress him, show him she could just have fun. She was up for just having fun.

She hadn't at first realized it was Amelia Miller, of course. Ms. Perry, hearing the vomiting, had been caught off-guard. Was that somehow she *herself* throwing up?

Amelia came out of the bathroom stall, wiping at her cheeks. Her clavicle jutted forward like pleading hands.

Ms. Perry was swallowing and swallowing.

It wasn't fair to view a student as a nemesis. Ms. Perry knew that. But Amelia Miller was more virus than girl, contaminating the rest of the class, who crowded around her at lunchtime, their bodies humming like cars about to start, decked out in cheap jewelry and colorful hairbands and patterned knee socks, asserting the differences belied by their uniforms. They wanted diet tips. They wanted to know, Were their lunches healthy? And Amelia Miller would look from lunch to lunch. Nope, nope, and...nope. She would then pick up a clammy slice of turkey, roll it into a kind of flower, and bite off its head.

Amelia, standing before Ms. Perry, was wearing the jewelry, the hairband, the knee socks. But on her they looked staged, as though her mother had dressed her.

It was a terrible thing, not to have a faculty bathroom.

"Amelia," said Ms. Perry. "Is there something you need to tell me?"

Ms. Perry reminded herself of her own mother, hands on hips.

"I have the flu," said Amelia. There were broken veins scattered across her face, gathering especially at the eyes, like premature crow's feet.

Her face was bloated as a drowned person's.

Ms. Perry could hold it in no longer. Luckily, there was the sink.

"*I* have the flu," said Ms. Perry. She wiped her mouth with a brown paper towel folded neatly in half.

Of all the things she saw—Sophie Bloom idly picking her nose in the hallway; Jane Nelson with a poorly-covered-up hickey on her neck, which she admitted was the result of a bicycle pump taken to her face in an ill-fated experiment; Lisa Carter with blood at the seat of her skirt, and many, many midriffs, proudly announcing themselves when ooh-oohing hands shot up in the air—this was the only she'd been obligated to report. But the trouble was the trouble it would take. She'd have to go to the principal, whose fear of computers complicated her life ridiculously. Among other absurdities, he still mandated handwritten report cards. She couldn't figure it out. Was it maybe supposed to be charming? A bold expression of OCD? She didn't know where he even got his carbon paper.

She'd have to go to the guidance counselor, who kept boxes of Special K in her office and a Weight Watchers point system pinned to her cork bulletin board. The guidance counselor was forever wanting to share with Ms. Perry what she'd eaten so far that day and how many Weight Watcher points she had left and how good she was being. The guidance counselor was fat in a doughy way, with an undifferentiated shelf of breast that made her seem pushy and obnoxious even when she was just sitting in her desk, quietly munching from a carefully measured-out baggie of Special K. Those were breasts that would charge at you in a crowded store or parking lot: Out of my way!

The guidance counselor would probably just be jealous. Bulimia, she would say. I used to have bulimia. Or anorexia, or a binge-eating disorder. The guidance counselor could get competitive when it came to conversations.

So Ms. Perry had made a deal with Amelia: Don't come down with the flu again, and no one will have to know.

It hadn't occurred to Ms. Perry—what was the matter with her?—that Amelia might tell on *her* for suspicious during-the-day vomiting.

The principal had called her into his office and shut the door. He was concerned, he told her. But the corners of his eyes were pinched tight, and really he was saying, I'm going to fire you. Ms. Perry found herself entirely out of options. Now, if she were to buck up and report Amelia, it would look petty, an unimaginative tit for Amelia's tat.

Ms. Perry began to speak too quickly, her words tumbling over each other like kindergarteners on their way to recess. She would have told him sooner, she explained—much too quickly! Why couldn't she slow down?— but she was waiting until the end of the first trimester. Better safe.

It occurred to her only later that the flu really was the best lie, and the most obviously there for the taking. There was something wrong with her, Ms. Perry knew. Her own teachers had accused her imagination of over-activity, and here it was: fidgeting, on the move, racing too far ahead.

The principal's blush spread even to his scalp, where stray wisps were arranged to approximate hair. He asked her if she needed to lie down. For a moment Ms. Perry panicked. Had she somehow said, I have cancer? Had she given the impression she was dying?

"Sometimes women in your"—he stopped to look at the ceiling—"condition find they need to lie down." He mimed a pregnant belly, his hand beginning at his chest, swooping far into the air, ending dangerously close to his crotch.

"I don't need to lie down," she said.

"All right," he said. "That's all right."

"The first trimester is almost done?" he asked.

She assured him it was.

"We don't discriminate here." His eyes darted up to meet hers, and then away, quickly as squirrels. "That's just something we don't do here. These are modern times," he told her, shaking his head as though confused.

But it would have been preferable if Ms. Perry were married. This was something the principal, very unfortunately, couldn't deny. This was a private, all-girls' school, it really couldn't be helped. There were certain expectations. There were certain standards. It was necessary, then, to have a plan of action in place before Ms. Perry publically confronted the rumors that had now spread from girl to girl like lice. A truth might perhaps have to stretch. The principal's hands, fisted, pulled slowly at the air.

So: Ta-da! Voila!

Ms. Perry was married now!

Her students—the ones who loved her—had at first been sad to find out they hadn't been invited to the wedding, or at least alerted to the news. And she was pregnant?

Hel-lo! Had they missed something?

But they were all past this now: They wished she were *their* mother!

There was still the lingering question of Ms. Perry's rings, and so she went to a costume jewelry store and pointed through a glass case to a ring with a small cubic zirconia diamond that looked like a snowflake.

"I don't know if I would," said the salesgirl. "Those things look like engagement rings." She made a quick slice at her throat. "Totally tacky."

"Oh," said Ms. Perry. "It's not for me. I mean, yes, it's for me, but it's for a costume. I'm going to be in a play."

The salesgirl was wearing earrings made of beads and trailing feathers that brushed her shoulders when she lifted them in a double shrug.

Ms. Perry began feeling desperate, as though she had to pee, and badly.

"I'm not in a play. I'm illegitimately pregnant and I teach at a backwards all-girls' school, and my principal wants me to pretend I'm married."

Ms. Perry found she believed herself. She summoned a single blooming tear.

The salesgirl put her hand to her mouth. Her nails were painted a careful magenta, and they spread across her face like a dried-out novelty starfish. "No way," she said. "That's like…"

"I know!" said Ms. Perry.

"You should sue," the salesgirl said. "That's what I would do, no question. I'd just sue his ass and live off the settlement."

"I would," Ms. Perry said. "But I've got to think about the baby." She gestured vaguely. "These court cases drag on," she said. "Even when they're open-shut."

And now, awfully, she mimed opening and shutting a door.

But the salesgirl seemed not to notice. "It's hard on single moms," she said. The beads in her earrings rattled.

Ms. Perry smiled with one side of her face, like a stroke victim.

The salesgirl came out from behind the glass counter and touched Ms. Perry's arm. Her breath smelled of spearmint and waxy strawberry. "I wish I could give this to you for free," she said.

But she could give Ms. Perry complimentary wrapping. She used silk ribbons, crisscrossed them, looping the remaining ribbon into a bow. She looked Ms. Perry in the eye. "This is how they do it at Tiffany's."

If Ms. Perry squinted and held her hand far from her face, her hand was transformed entirely. She was someone she hadn't realized she'd wanted to be. Of course! It was so obvious now. Marriage was the ticket.

Married and pregnant, she was intoxicating to be around. Her students gazed up at her during her lessons, pupils enlarged, as though stumbling from darkened rooms. Sophie Bloom's eyes crossing more consistently than was usual.

Tell us the story! they demanded.

They interrupted the lessons: So was his family like the Capulets or the Montagues? Was he more of a Mercutio or a real, hunky Romeo? They hoped Romeo, but were pragmatic enough to account for this other possibility.

What was she going to name the baby?

And because she was a pushover, a teacher who was also kind of a friend, having failed to follow the advice she'd been given by any and all who heard she was to teach (never smile for the first month!), she made up stories for them.

She had direction, a purpose, as never before. She was not, anymore, just someone who chiefly corrected spellings: Lose; not loose. Comma; not coma, getting mixed up herself, scribbling on their papers, making arrows and asterisks and smiley faces: Never mind!

No longer did she sit in her apartment, watching teenybopper TV shows whose titles she carefully messed up if ever they should come up in conversation with people who were not her students. *Dawson's Lake?* she'd say, and laugh and call herself a dork when corrected: No, no: it was *Dawson's Creek.*

She prepared all the W and one H questions with an intellectual rigor she'd forgotten all about. It was like finding an old picture of herself. Oh yes, that was her, wasn't it?

His name was Sebastian. He was a lawyer. They'd met on the street—it was so funny!—he'd literally run into her. And she'd dropped all her papers—their *Lord of the Flies* essays, in fact. And he picked them up, and then, well, he'd picked her up. He'd used all the hardest vocabulary words: Can I at least take you out for coffee to make up for my boorishness, my obstreperousness, my inanity?

It had all happened so suddenly. She'd been swept utterly off her feet.

The how of it was the only question that stumped her. How *did* it happen? How did one go from coffee and empty pleasantries to a whole life spent with this other person?

"It's ineffable," she told her students.

This satisfied them not all. They were like fact-checkers, scouring for details. "Sebastian, like the lobster from *The Little Mermaid?*" asked Susan Lee.

Actually, it was exactly like that. *The Little Mermaid* had been playing on a loop over the weekend, and Ms. Perry had somehow ended up watching it twice. That was just like her. Most everything that came to her was revealed, ultimately, as a thought someone else had had first.

"Did you get married because of the baby?" Amy Heller asked, her eyes wide and glassy with contact lenses that had only days ago replaced her glasses.

"Rude," hissed Lisa Carter. Hissing, but smiling also. Because the answer seemed terribly clear.

"Actually, no," said Ms. Perry. "We got married quickly because his mother is dying, and he wanted her to be at the wedding. And we're hoping—we're really hoping—she'll get to see the new baby, too."

She'd heard this story somewhere before, but she couldn't place it. Was it maybe the plot of a made-for-TV movie? Something she'd read in *Glamour* magazine? It had the distinct ring of a story one of her student might have written for the brief and painful creative writing unit, which had to be unceremoniously cut short when Lucy Philips handed in a story titled "Guns are Good".

Ms. Perry's story, if it were a missing cat, would be one of those listed as, Without any distinguishing features.

But her girls seemed, strangely, to believe her. They were sighing and nodding, foreheads creasing with worry, with love. It was so romantic! It was really brave, also. And, like, was the wedding in her hospital room? Did Ms. Perry need to wear a veil and also a hospital mask? All the nurses, probably, were clapping, right? And were there so many flowers some had to be donated to sick kids or to people without enough visitors?

What was Sebastian's mother dying of?

For a moment, Ms. Perry felt like asking, Who? But then she remembered: Sebastian, the boorish, obstreperous, inane, apologetic, romantic, sincere, hunky Romeo of man, was her husband. Ms. Perry lowered her eyes. "Emphysema," she whispered. "From smoking in high school."

Sophie Bloom lingered one day after class, slowly, slowly dropping her pencils into her pencil case. One. Another. Another. Amelia Miller stood behind her, a presence to be ignored. If Ms. Perry spoke to Sophie long enough, Amelia would give up. She, surely, had a bus to catch, a mother waiting in a mini-van.

"Sophie," Ms. Perry said. "What's up?"

Sophie shrugged. "The sky," she said, but without her usual oomph.

Ms. Perry sat at the edge of her desk with her feet dangling. All her favorite teachers had had feet that dangled from desks.

"I made you something," said Sophie, shrugging. "In art class, I did."

"How lovely," said Ms. Perry.

"It's just"— and Sophie's face became extremely scrunched— "I just really hope your baby turns out to be a girl."

She rummaged through her knapsack, which stank, Ms. Perry couldn't overlook, of overripe cantaloupe. Sophie pulled out a tiny pink hat. "My older sister says it's bad luck," she said. "To plan in advance."

"In advance?" said Ms. Perry.

"In advance of the baby." Sophie twirled a strand of hair around her finger so the tip went white. "Because you never know about these things."

Sophie's eyes seemed to kiss, then parted, embarrassed strangers. It would not be a lie to say Ms. Perry loved Sophie Bloom.

"I don't believe in bad luck," said Ms. Perry. "And Sophie is my grandmother's name, actually. If it's a girl, that's what we'll name her, Sophie."

Sophie looked at the floor and beamed.

Amelia Miller, still there, said, "Ms. Perry?"

A deep breath in, out. "I'm talking to Sophie," Ms. Perry said.

"It's okay," said Sophie. "That was it."

And Ms. Perry was forced to collect herself, make a kind of

smile. "I only have a few minutes," she told Amelia. "So you've got to make it quick."

Amelia nodded. Her face had taken on a kind of Victorian pallor, her skin stretched taut over the hollows of her cheeks. She looked old, but also, from certain angles, much too young. Not for her were the awkward buds of breasts held in place, even if they didn't yet quite need to be, with bras adorned with tiny ribbons, flowers that poked through uniform shirts like oddly misplaced nipples. Or sports bras for the more embarrassed, worn backwards, in Lisa Carter's case, in a terrible, poignant attempt to hide what was becoming clear. Amelia was entirely flat. It was even possible that she wore an undershirt instead of a bra.

"I didn't realize you were pregnant," Amelia said. "It seemed like something else. Like, the smell. I think gin."

Ms. Perry's laughter sounded like it came from a cartoon: ha ha ha.

She wasn't going to ask Amelia how she knew what gin smelled like. Where was everyone else? Where was the guidance counselor, the principal who cared so much? And what about, for god's sake, the other teachers? Was she really the only one who noticed what was going on? It was so clear it might have come from a psych 101 textbook: an introverted, upper-middle class, white, preteen girl with problems at home.

There had been girls like Amelia in Ms. Perry's high school, though none in middle school, she didn't think. Actually, now that she was thinking of it, there might have only been one girl. There was Ms. Perry's imagination again, overacting, multiplying when it should be staying out of the way and still. The girl—it was just the one, Ms. Perry was sure now—had been a kind of celebrity in the school. Every so often, she'd be hospitalized, and then return looking normal, but not really. The normalcy was only temporary, worn like a new, ill-fitting dress. Soon enough she'd be thin again, very and then ghastly. One day, she came to school with a tube in her nose. And she was so nice, so friendly. Always smiling, even with that tube, even with the strips of healed or healing cuts that braceleted her wrists. It was possible that she'd ending up dying. There might have been an email.

"Well, clearly it wasn't gin," Ms. Perry said now to Amelia. "It's dangerous to drink while you're pregnant. Don't they teach you anything in Health?"

She hadn't meant to ask a question.

"We talk about healthy eating," Amelia said. "We learned about the food pyramid."

"That's nice," said Ms. Perry.

"I know a lot about it," Amelia said. "Because of my diet, so."

Ms. Perry had to say something. She had to.

"That's nice," she repeated.

Amelia looked at her scabbed knuckles.

"Your mother must be waiting," Ms. Perry said.

"My babysitter," said Amelia.

"Well, a babysitter shouldn't have to wait!" Ms. Perry was all but shouting. She was all but smiling.

Amelia heaved her knapsack onto her thin, breakable shoulders.

Ms. Perry had been in awe of the girl in her high school. How controlled she was, how good. Once, Ms. Perry had tried to starve herself, but by dinnertime she was so hungry she couldn't see straight. She liked to eat. There it was. In a fury, another time, she'd smashed the glass frame of a portrait her grandmother had painted of her. The symbolism, she'd thought at the time, was profound. She'd made a scratch along her wrist, but she couldn't bring herself to dig deep enough to draw blood.

Ms. Perry missed her bus and had to wait.

The sky had turned an oily kind of gray, the color of pigeon wings. She liked who she became under this sky: a harried, youngish wife who was keeping her husband waiting. A wife whose husband, Sebastian, would yell at her and then apologize. He would put his big hand on her belly and, tears in his eyes, tell her it was just that he was afraid of how enormously everything was about to change. She would understand. I know, she'd say. I know, but we're in this together.

The next bus was so packed there were no bars to hold onto, and so Ms. Perry was held upright, it felt, by strangers' bodies. There was someone's arm thrust against her breast, someone else leaning into the small of her back. Ms. Perry might not have been there at all. Just across from her was a pregnant woman, seated and beatific.

Ms. Perry twisted her engagement ring so the fake diamond pressed against her palm. She twirled it back around. Now it caught some florescent light.

"When's the baby due?" Ms. Perry said.

The woman lifted her pocketbook to her lap.

"I'm just a few weeks in," said Ms. Perry. She put her hand to her stomach. Oh little plum. Oh tiny, blushing, feathery sprite. This was what it was not to be lonely.

The pregnant woman smiled. She was Ms. Perry's best friend now. "I'm at the point where, when I stand up, I don't want to sit down. I might not be able to get up the next time! But of course, everyone gives up their seat for you once you're showing so enormously. And, right, that's not even when you need a seat. When you need a seat is right in the beginning, when just breathing makes you nauseous."

There was no heaving or panting, but a sudden, simple lifting. "Please," she said, waving majestically. "Have my seat."

It became time to hand in report cards. The principal left a detailed letter in Ms. Perry's faculty mailbox. The letter was printed on grainy white stationary that had a weight like no other paper. The principal outlined the due dates and expectations, ending on a jubilant note of faith in her abilities as a tough-but-fair educator. All the other teachers had identical envelopes tucked into their mailboxes. He believed strongly in the personal touch.

Ms. Perry's students didn't receive letter grades, but numbers, ranging from one (unthinkable!) to four (she was not supposed to, officially, award them as cavalierly as she did). She decided she'd go to the faculty break room during lunch so she could copy her grades onto to the carbon paper against the copy machine's sputtering whirr, which might pass, in moments of severe desperation, for postmodern music.

The guidance counselor stopped her in the hallway. She plucked the carbon paper from Ms. Perry's arms. "You don't want to unduly exert yourself."

She pretended to stagger beneath the thin stack of paper.

"I swear, I'd never guess you were pregnant," she said. "Boy, when I was pregnant, my bust went straight one way, my bottom the opposite!" The guidance counselor became suddenly serious. "I gained a great deal of weight. A great deal. It's not a favor to anyone to stay thin during your pregnancy."

And then her face lit with sudden delight: "To *try* to stay thin."

Her hand shot out and was now patting Ms. Perry's stomach, just between her hipbones, where period cramps came to congregate. Ms. Perry thought of pro-choice campaigns: Leave my uterus alone!

She stepped backward.

The guidance counselor looked as close as she ever could to concerned. "You're, what would it be now, four months along?"

All Ms. Perry could think to do was agree.

She smiled a doll's smile, all mouth and no eyes. She was reminded of being a child: Alarm, alarm, she and her brother used to bleat, running from imaginary robbers, so breathless it hurt to breathe.

She left the carbon papers with the guidance counselor, laughing in a kind of way, and went to find the principal. His door was all the way open, held in place by a dictionary that was terrifically thick. He had an open door policy, he liked to say. He called for her to come on in and not at all to be shy.

She was not feeling, she said, her best.

He mimed the pregnancy he imagined for her.

She made her lips a line and nodded.

The principal was at once on his feet, tiny springs maybe really beneath his wingtip shoes. He all but slung her over his back and out of the office, as though she were a bag of recyclables, or a bride.

Ms. Perry did some research and found a four-month-term fetus would have bendable bones, fur, a light marbling of fat. And it could kick. She had gone wrong somewhere, but she couldn't figure out how to retrace her steps, locate her former self, shake her, stop her in the act. Because here she was, no different from her students, getting caught up with some fad, some hobby, getting obsessed, and then forgetting. *Not forgetting.* The pregnancy had become like a pimple: She was aware of it, it worried her, but for now, she was going to let it sit.

She lost the baby.

And her husband, boorish and perfect, abandoned her. Her mother-in-law went into shock and died. Ms. Perry removed her ring.

She called the principal. He offered condolences. He told her the students would make her a card. He told her there would be a sub, not to worry. She drew the shades in her apartment, sat quietly on the bed, head in hand, as though there were something real for her to mourn.

The thing to do was call her friend Jeff. They weren't friends, really. Or, they had once been friends. But then they'd almost dated, after his girlfriend had told him she loved him but he wasn't smart enough to be her husband. Ms. Perry had thought, at the time, Well, why not. But after the one date, she'd stopped answering his calls. So he surprised her, came to her apartment uninvited, with grocery store flowers, said he thought he loved her, or could love her. Thanks, but she was pretty busy, she'd said. He should really call, if he was going to come over. They hadn't spoken for months after that, but then they ran into each over at a party and pretended nothing had ever happened. And then she fell into the habit of sometimes going to his apartment, which was dirty and cold and narrow, though with multiple rooms. Jeff didn't have a steady job, but he kept himself in the money by renting out rooms in his apartment for triple their worth. That was what he said, anyway. His parents might have been supporting him.

He told her, now, to come on over, sure.

On the bus, she held herself gingerly, shoulders straight.

No one gave her a seat. Those seats weren't for her. There was a pregnant woman on the bus—there were pregnant women everywhere, it turned out—gazing out the window, eyes bovine and glassy. Another woman sat with a little boy on her lap, the stroller precariously balanced against the wall next to them. The boy had white-blond hair that fell partway over his eyes. His nose was running. Her boy would have had a haircut; he wouldn't have gotten a cold.

When she got there, Jeff offered her water. The water was from the tap and came in a smudged, dirty glass. She imagined she saw the ghost of another woman's lipstick, though she knew Jeff didn't go for women who wore lipstick, and also that it didn't matter. She wasn't his wife. He wasn't her husband.

"Don't you ever do the dishes?" she said.

"Yes, I do, thanks for asking, *Mom*," he said.

She became a cartoon again: ha ha ha.

When she was done with her water, he cut his toenails. It was an unrelated activity, he told her. He'd been planning to cut them even before she called. "I do the deed in the bathroom," he explained, inviting her to follow him in. "More sanitary."

She politely acted not horrified by the bathroom. Chunks were missing from the walls, mold blossoming along the edges of the tub. Two cockroaches perched on the edge of the sink like a pair of doves. There didn't appear to be a toothbrush. Jeff hummed a non-tune as he clipped off the yellow whirls into the rust-outlined toilet. The hair on his toes, she noticed, was black, mossy, edging into the territory of gorilla. It wasn't like she could ask him to shave it. But *she* did. She shaved her toes.

He brought her into the bedroom, where there was a pile of dirty laundry stacked high enough in one corner that it was possible, from a distance, to mistake for a soft chair. She dead-fished it on the bed, head to the ceiling, a little floppy on the bumpy mattress, but basically still. He unhooked her bra, idly twirled his fingers around her nipples. He told her, as he always did, that she had great boobs. She told him, as she always did, that she really preferred he call them "breasts." He moved in to suck.

"Okay," she said. "Good work. That's enough."

He wanted to know what the problem was. He always wanted to know what the problem was.

But what was she supposed to say? Don't remind me of my baby, who's not real? Don't be a man who's not my husband, who's also not real?

"You just seemed sort of like a vampire for second there," she said. "Also, you've got a water stain up there shaped like an amoeba."

He needed to turn over to see the ceiling. He didn't say anything, but then he laughed, a little, haltingly, like it was his second language. He told her she was a piece of work, one weird girl, did she know that?

Her students had already been briefed by the time she returned. The guidance counselor had given a talk, Sophie Bloom told Ms. Perry in a voice soft as powder. Ms. Perry had perfectly prepared the story. She'd practiced. But they would not ask her how it had happened, what had been said. They sat at their desks like the students she'd imagined before she began teaching, moveable pieces of chess. They sat and stared at her, some with little girl legs spread unwittingly apart, others already crossed at the knees or ankles. They seemed simple and small enough to hold. And there was Amelia, gray pouches under her eyes, looking sad and understanding.

OLD FOR YOUR AGE,
TALL FOR YOUR HEIGHT

No one dared reach for a cookie. They were on diets, they said, politely. Because they could imagine—Victoria's mother, bent pragmatically over a bowl, the sticky mound rising up from the spaces between her fingers, slickly sucking. It gave them, seriously, *the chills*. They murmured their thank-you-anyways. She didn't say anything, just still stood there, arms outstretched with her cookies on a tray. The way she was looking at them, they three might have been the cut-outs of movie stars or Olympic ice-skaters with which their bedroom walls were plastered, Karin's held in place by folded-over Band-Aids, because her family was forever out of tape.

Victoria's mother smiled without her teeth.

And yes, it was sad to see her standing there, smiling, but Karin thought Victoria's mother's life was easier than their mothers made it out to be, back in their houses, where they flipped through a rolodex of how-would-you-likes and could-you- imagines, and Stella's mother, who was always having one or another breakdown, spat selfish-selfishs after them, catapulting perfectly as Molly's brothers' softballs.

"You girls don't need to be on diets," Victoria's mother said, and put down the cookies. She wrapped her hands in her skirt.

They ducked their heads with no answer for her. They weren't really on diets. The bottoms of their backpacks were right then padded with smashed chips wadded in plastic, tightly tied.

Store-bought sandwich cookies they knew how to turn exactly, like clocks, for all the cream to stay on one side. They only even knew about diets vaguely, from their older sisters, who, on grim-faced nights before school, stuffed Tupperware containers with lettuce, making off with their mothers' bottles of vinegar.

Karin had once walked in on Amelia in the bathroom, where she sat, knees to chin on the toilet, eating turkey slices with her fingers. She lifted each clammy piece from its center, shoving the folds of turkey in her mouth all at once. Karin didn't talk about it with them. Their sisters were not quite theirs to discuss. They used other bathrooms if it came to that, and together only compared the goose bumps they got thinking of Victoria, where they cut lines into the dustings of hair, made them stand almost straight. Except for Molly's arms, since she'd shaved them, on a dare, or not on a dare. Her arms, before, had been hairy as her brothers'.

Victoria's mother's smile shifted just a bit, as if some photographer had asked her to arrange it this way, please. "Victoria is always so happy when you girls come. She's been looking forward all day."

Improbable, and their cue. They fell over each other to stand up. Some of the frizz from Molly's ponytail landed on Karin's lips, a whisper of a spider web that made her flinch, as though Molly's hair belonged to a stranger. They trotted out of the kitchen, enough behind Victoria's mother not to seem like they were following her, really.

Victoria's mother opened the door to her room with such care.

"Vee-vee," she called, sweetly. "Look who's come to see you." And, pitched so high, because maybe still this way was easiest for Victoria's tiny ears to process, "Your friends, darling."

Victoria was standing up in her crib, fists wrapping the bars. Her hair was gathered in a wispy puff of half-pony. She had the oversized head of a regular baby, the nearly eye-reaching cheeks, the satin skin. Her elbows and knees were creased in slight rings when she didn't move them to kick or reach. There was something glaring that made her not look like a regular baby, but nothing they could ever point at or to. Looking at her made Karin feel almost dizzy with wanting, and absolutely not wanting, to blow a raspberry into Victoria's belly. It wasn't right! Karin was forever on the edge of screaming out. Hands a fan in someone's face, Hello?

Victoria was their duty. That much they understood. She would have been one of them, their mothers were forever saying, impervious to their thrown-back heads. They meant, Victoria was their age. She was she was well within the cut-off, an April baby. She would've been in their class, no question. It made Karin think, in a hazy, wrong way, of her father's back from parent-teacher conference joke about her sister: "Well, it's just your run-of-the-mill case of being old for your age and tall for your height."

But nonetheless, Wednesdays, Victoria days, woke in them, each time, a kind of frustrated wonder anew: Why them? Why now? Because hadn't they, for years, been the age everyone said Victoria was? They were old enough, was all their mothers ever said, pressing them out their doors, lunch bags ready or not. They ought to.

So there they were, Wednesday after Wednesday.

Victoria stared up at them now, as she always did, before opening into a smile that showed her teeth. They were real, adult teeth, ridged at the bottom like their sisters' saltine crackers.

They called out their pleasantries. They were nice girls,

weren't they? Karin's mother was always checking. When they went out? The three of them? It made Karin proud to be asked, as if they were another kind of group, attracted to one another despite circumstance, and because of some quality she couldn't in general define. They'd come together, instead, through the hard work and social sieving of their sisters, who were friends for reasons she'd never thought to analyze, any more than she'd ever wondered why her parents were married to, of all people, each other. They'd never had to approach each other and ask for a mall date, or however other girls did it. Never had they lain in their beds, eyes trained to ceiling, wondering, with white-knuckled, bit-lipped austerity, Does she like me? They were all just there, scenery in the rooms of their sisters. But sometimes their mothers forgot, Karin's especially, and mistook them, maybe, for their older sisters. They wanted them, foreheads lined, to be nice. As if the choice was theirs to make!

They stood on tiptoe and cooed.

Stella's mother picked them up. They weren't allowed to walk anymore, because of all the freshly cropped-up signs about the predator on the loose—*sexual*, their sisters had sing-songed when their mothers left it just at *predator* to their fathers. The complex of houses they thought of as just Victoria's, especially, was a better-not-to. Just beyond the cheerfully painted, ruffled-curtained houses was a forest where, it was common knowledge, teenagers went to do their drugs, and bad things could happen.

It was only ever Stella's mother or Karin's mother picking up, because Molly's mother worked and also there were nine children in Molly's family. "She's not doing anything a rat can't do," Karin's mother always said after Molly's mother had another baby. The latest baby was a boy. Gabriel Gabriel Gabriel. Karin sang it in her mind like a song.

Stella's sister was switching seats with her mother when they got in the car. "Thanks, now I'll never learn to drive," she said to them.

Stella leaned all the way forward. "You're welcome."

The winter sun caught Stella's hair at the part and made Karin feel proud. But then, no, she took the feeling back: That hair was Stella's, and hers was something different.

Stella's mother said, "Seatbelts, or your mothers will kill me."

Not really. Molly and Karin looked at each other.

Their mothers, all together, were always saying, Isn't it nice, Aren't we lucky, and, The way all our kids get along, but then in their cars, there would sometimes be these other things they said. Their mothers' eyes might get narrow or wide, their voices high and girlish, or very low, so they almost had to lean in to hear.

Karin slid her fingers under her thighs. The leather was warm but dry, because of how cold outside was. She loved being in the car when it was like this. The smell was lipstick and pine air freshener.

"How's the baby," Stella's mother said.

Karin got both elbows, cheeks hot against hers, scratchy with winter hats and scarves, and their breath. They were all probably picturing Victoria, the way they'd sat for the hour they were supposed to, filling her in on the weather, the way Karin knew how the most from grandparents who came from far to visit, and then on jokes they'd heard, mostly from Molly's older brothers. They imitated their teacher and the quiet way she paced the classroom, the seat of her slacks perennially stained with chalk. In their neatly arranged semi-circle of chairs, they held themselves stiff, scoliosis-preventative-straight. They reached under their blouses to make their armpits fart.

And, in between, they tried to tell themselves: Our age. Our age. Or, Baby. Baby. Each required a kind of heartbeat of convincing. Neither was true. What girl their age, what tiny, drooling baby, would require a mother at the window, veined forehead peeking in, every so often, always?

Stella's mother looked back at them in the mirror.

"Molly's baby," she said. "My god, girls."

Molly breathed in to speak, but Karin was bored of listening to the same old we-can't-sleep, He-wakes-up-five-times-a-night. The lampposts and telephone poles were all marked with mimeographed warnings. She couldn't read them as they breezed past, but she had them memorized. They were to be careful of: phone calls from people they didn't know. Stopping for strange cars with rolled-down windows. Being out alone. Especially if they were girls.

In the sketch his hair was droopy and straight, a spider plant fallen over his forehead. His eyes glinted with small white flashes—"To make him look all the more nefarious," Karin's father had said, winking elaborately at her mother. And then, "No, no. Probably his terrible powers know no limits." Smiling, his hand a quick sandpaper rub to stubbled chin. Karin's mother had laughed in a fake, mean way. "Tell that to the parents of Allison Eve Johnson."

Allison Eve Johnson was on papers also, a real, smiling picture. "MISSING" was lettered just above the sharp part in her scalp where someone had made her braids. At first Karin couldn't understand why she would be smiling so hard in the picture. It wasn't so bad, if she could smile, and Karin felt a desperate kind of misunderstanding. Why was it so bad? Why, if she was smiling? Amelia had looked at her like she was a headache crept just behind her eyes. That picture was from *before*.

They dropped off Stella's sister on the way. She got out of the car without looking at them, ponytail wagging between her shoulder blades, like a finger saying, Don't come here, but really, Come here. Her boots left perfect tracks in the snow.

"Awfully quiet over there, Karin," Stella's mother said. She found Karin's eyes in the mirror. Spittle or toothpaste crusted her lips, just at the corners. Karin would have been embarrassed if she was her mother, but she wasn't her mother, and so Karin loved her.

She shrugged, smiling. "We told her we were on diets."

"Told who?" Stella's mother squinted in the mirror. "You girls are dieting?"

Stella brought her knees to her chin. Molly was examining the holes in her arms where the hair used to be. No one, they said. No.

The rest of the week lobbed slippery variables at them, a cascade of ifs and thens, questions disguised as comments, tests at every corner to fail—When were their bedtimes, Sheila Heller, on Friday wanted to know, cheeks illuminated as if with fever, arches delicate in their side-to-side wobble, and when they proffered, proudly, their fabricated answers (would they were girls with bedtimes!) she ponytail-bobbed away, laughing, screeching, Babies!

But on Wednesday the flickering tendons in their necks went tight. They became hard-knocked prairie girls ducking their heads in deference, clutching aprons in modest curtseys revealing the most sturdy of boots, laced. They wiped their palms ready. And if their siblings didn't understand? If their parents saw them only from the corners of their eyes, shadows to the wall, if, say, in Molly's house, the baby was red with crying and the toddler was too, and in, say, Karin's house, her mother and Amelia were fighting over the ladder of bones poking through her sister's back—because unlike the others, she never broke her diet—and Karin's father was joking, and Stella's mother, in her house, was pacing for the possibility of a child out in the rain without adequate gear? If that? They had their duty. Carried to their chests like flowers at a wedding, not yet ready to be thrown.

They hurried, harried, from their classrooms.

The letdown was always the same. Victoria's mother, smiling her perfectly lipsticked smile, soft hands at their backs, ushering them inside. How was their day? she wanted to know, like some mother out of the movies. Where was her collie dog and apron? they'd laugh among themselves, sometimes, after.

Victoria's father had left, years and years ago, though still not just after she was born. Presumably, he'd tried and found it wasn't for him, this business of being forever an infant's father. They could understand, absolutely. Stella and Karin joked— Molly's father should've left too! He was also never without a baby! They were allowed to joke like that, mostly. They weren't friends because they necessarily liked each other, and that was what it meant, they would never say out loud, that they were closest to sisters.

The hallways at Victoria's were free from family pictures, and what a good thing. A picture might have been taken ten years ago or one and there was no polite way to ask. Instead, Victoria's mother hung paintings of triangles and squiggles that Stella's mother said once, to them, Victoria must have painted herself. Karin thought they were kind of nice. She could just imagine a gallery of people peering carefully at the canvases, hands to chins, murmuring, aloud or in thought, Triangles.

Squiggles. Oh yes. The exact opposite of Karin's mother, whose answer to Karin's questions was every time, "You know, I don't know."

This week Victoria's mother had celery waiting. The logs glistened, shreds of green hanging off some edges. It would be like hair to swallow.

Victoria's mother opened her hand to the finely water-dappled plate as if revealing some fantastic magic trick. "Since you girls are dieting."

They had no choice, and never did, at Victoria's.

Their necks, without even their telling them to, tilted just to the side, just a little, as they called out their thank-yous, you-didn't-have-tos. They sat around the table, careful to still their knees. Their days were fine. No—they were excellent. They had: Gym! Biology! Their jaws ached as if with too much candy.

"It's so wonderful, girls, that you come to visit," she said. And then her lips made just the smallest sound. Like maybe the shy first beginning of a kiss. Her jaw moved for her to smile, as if, for her, it hurt and was hard.

"I'm just not sure," she said. She was looking at the table, where her hands were, knuckles poking sharply from that softly-lotioned skin. Karin noticed a small pale freckle, a floating piece of orzo.

"It's just that—" her contact lens glimmered in her eye. "Oh," she said, smiling. Shaking her head. She brought her finger up to her eye. The lens sat on her finger like a tiny bowl of iridescent dew. She looked at her finger, smooth and clean and long.

"It's just that, well, you girls must have your own lives."

They were still chewing her celery, strands weaving coolly into the cracks of their teeth, tangling in coils, Karin was sure, around the small brightly rubber-banded squares that hugged each of Molly's teeth, pressing down.

They reached the decision somehow without speaking. She didn't even *want* them. Their nods were quick, breathy sighs out. In the car, when Karin's mother asked, they chimed, hitting their various notes, Fine. They let the rest of the week dribble away as always, enduring, enduring: The awful indignities of being called up to the board in class, the tentative hands of their teacher squeezing encouragement to their shoulders, garlic breath all through the afternoon, and the general feeling that they might be coming down with breast cancer.

And, slowly, suddenly— Wednesday opened before them like a window. What freedom had fallen to them! The school bus spit them out on Victoria's lawn. They hoisted their knapsacks onto both shoulders. No one was watching: They could. Really, scoliosis was a fear drilled deeply into them, their having witnessed, with ample pinches of horror, Molly's oldest sister's two-year tenure in a brace. Alone and free, they realigned the bones in their backs, commanding, praying, Straight.

The lamppost signs seemed just then to flutter. Again, they didn't have to discuss it to know. She was a thumbprint over every photograph their minds could make, blurring every image peach. Allison Eve Johnson. They did not dare breathe her name aloud.

"She might be around here," Karin said. She felt happier than she had in maybe years.

"Her body," she said.

They compared arms for goose bumps. Molly's hair was growing back stubbly in a way that made Karin glad, and sure, she wasn't her.

"Probably the forest," Stella said. She shivered. Possibly it was not for show.

They didn't speak as they walked away from all the houses, into the forest. There was just the soft crunching of their boots over ice-crusted and blackened snow, the slight skid of their rubber heels on salt. Their breath ribboned out before them like misty shines of flashlight. All the leaves were covered. Above them, the trees were stripped and bony.

"Do you think he took her here?" Molly said, and, at their faces, their eyebrows rising up in obviously of course, she bounced back on her heels, the synthetic puff of her hood scratching her cold-rashed cheeks.

"I mean do you think he *took* her here. For stuff."

She eyed one mitten-linted fingernail elaborately before biting.

Stella and Karin looked away. Stuff. They knew only vague outlines beyond the clearly delineated facts to be found in the pink pamphlets pressed seriously into their palms after Sex Ed, which Stella's mother, laughing, had tossed away. Laughing why, they weren't sure. Because the strange glories and terrors described between those pages weren't true? Because were? They were, among the three of them, from big enough families: They weren't innocents. But when Karin tried to imagine Allison Eve Johnson and the predator, she could come up with only floating mimeographs of faces, the one grinning in a piano show of teeth.

Stella rubbed her knuckles just beneath her nose, where it was beginning to chap.

"Probably he said something first."

Their voices became cats slipping past each other.

"Like maybe, 'Come here, gorgeous.'"

"Or, 'Honey, you're so pretty.'"

"'I'd like to pop your cherry.'"

They paused, Karin picturing ice-cream sundaes, the round glisten on top, redolent, ripe.

They were a throat to sky chorus of Ewww.

But he would be gruff, also, they had to remember. He was a predator.

So: "'You get over here or else.'"

So a gun bulging from one worn denim pocket, greasy and cool to the touch. So pressed up against the temple of Allison Eve Johnson. And her parka ripped off, cotton stuffing everywhere, but buried by now, no one would find it. All the buttons of her school blouse, popped. Just her round collar kept miraculously intact, a rare winter butterfly spotted by a strong and chiseled boy just close by enough to save her. Her screams muffled by the deflated parka, and the boy, Karin could imagine him well, newspapers slung over his shoulder—though their newspapers were not delivered by boys on foot, but by men on trucks—only wondering idly at the hazily drifting butterfly, white as milk or bread.

They were breathless.

They fell back and made angels against the hardened snow, staring up at empty branches. They were laughing, and shy. Who knew? Who would have guessed, to look at them, three girls, the ends of their hair occasionally paintbrush-stiff from sucking, always in vaguely out of fashion hand-me-downs, what they did know? What they might imagine. Because, Allison Eve Johnson had been brutally, brutally, murdered, all signs pointed to, and they were laughing. They had *some nerve*, Karin could almost hear her mother saying. When would they *wake up and smell the coffee*?

Karin sat up, using her elbows and all the rest.

"What would the predator do if he found Victoria?"

Molly said something, but it was muffled from her still lying down. But they were done with lying down! They were sitting up now. Now they were talking about something else. Karin felt as if someone had taken a bicycle pump to her chest, and she wanted to feel something else. They were nice girls, their mothers said, the skin at their mouths tightly stretched, weren't they?

"Why don't you just sit up?" Karin said.

Stella said, "Hey, Karin," because of the way her voice got. It became just like her father's when he was maybe looking for something he couldn't find. So even. So calm.

"What?" she said. "What? I'm not doing anything."

Her spine was a twig that would not snap.

"You're such babies," she said. "Both of you. You don't understand." And then she had to stop speaking and start crying because she didn't either understand. Victoria was their age. That she was never going to grow up was not true. Her age was piling on and on, every day for her was also another.

Their hands were on her, patting, soothing: Shhhh. Because of course it was perfectly understandable, crying out in the frosted woods, a predator looming on the loose. She shook them off, shoulders tight to ears. The old snow-covered leaves were too ruined to crackle beneath her. If the predator found Victoria, she would be in the perfect disguise, a stooped and ugly witch really a swan-necked princess. Or the reverse. But the predator wouldn't find Victoria, not unless he went foot by careful foot up the unevenly placed bricks on the sides of what Karin's mother called, Oh, a *modern* house. Not unless he, with foresight-purchased tools, pried open the window, and entered. She was so safe. All this time, she had been so safe.

Karin's heart was in her ears. She found a tree to lean against.

The roots pressed up from the ground. Their hands were back, and they were laughing, pressing Reallys and Come-on-alreadys through the down, fingers pausing to tuck their stray grown-out-bangs behind ears, and then returning to her, hovering, uncertain now, just at the center of her back. Really, seriously, they wanted to go home. Wasn't Stella's mother waiting. Wouldn't Stella's mother be worried. But Karin was hearing Victoria's mother in her mind, that soft, lotion-smooth voice, You girls must have your own lives. And she felt, then, how Victoria's mother was afraid of them, and of what they were becoming.

CARE

They were in our yard. I watched them from the window, the son's mushroom cap of hair lifting, electric in the wind, the wife without her shoes. I listened to her shout, Max. Max! Sun caught her stockings and made them glisten. I'd never seen the son off his leash before. They were perfect: husband, wife, son. She was a cellist, the wife. I saw her leave the house sometimes with the case, sheets of music fluttering in the breeze. I didn't know what the husband did. I imagined something wonderful. Lion tamer.

They had nothing to do with us.

We were having breakfast.

Amelia patted butter into her socks. She was fantastic at it. She didn't have to look down. She made perfect eye contact with our mother, nodding. Yes. And, Interesting. Her hand all this time down her sock, smearing.

My mother was saying, "It doesn't matter as much when it's summer. No one does anything when it's summer."

She meant the plans Amelia and I hadn't managed. Dr. Feingold said, Absolutely, Amelia needs to have summer plans. He also said Amelia would die if she stayed out of the hospital. Maybe not today, he'd said, leaning forward, fingers steepled exactly.

He was just a regular doctor—he still tried to give us lollipops, even Amelia. We were asking too much of him, he said. And my parents said, yes, they knew. But now they were trying an at home approach.

My father passed me the milk. It poured out close to clear.

"This tastes like water," I said. Amelia kicked me under the table.

"So strange," I said. I kicked her back.

"I'm sure it's fine," my father said. He knocked a fist to his lips.

I cut into the stack of pancakes my mother had set out for everyone.

No one laughed. "Mom," I said. I waved my fork.

"Good," my mother said. "It's good to see you girls eating."

I knocked back my chair, slammed it three times to the wall, indenting already-indentations. The family was gone. The wife had captured the son somehow while I wasn't watching. She'd brought him back inside. And there they would eat a careless breakfast of cereal, standing up. Over the sink.

My father put his hands on my shoulders. Pressed. "I love you," he said.

He kissed me just above my head. I felt it on my spine. My mother was with Amelia, telling her goodbye, and then they switched, my mother's kiss smudging onto my cheek, my father's hands on Amelia's bones.

We love you too, we told them.

And then they were gone, and I was here, so watching her. Watching her! She was my older sister. I missed the way it used to be, when she lived in the eating disorder unit of the hospital, a feeding tube taped many times to her nose, tangles of wires tracking the rhythms of her murmuring heart. She'd seemed like a kind of ambassador then, introducing me to the world she lived in so easily, her paper gown fluttering around her like a cape. And even though the other girls, with their caved-in faces, seemed related to her, I was the only one who was actually her sister.

"Hey," she said now. "Check this out."

She unzipped the sweatshirt she wore as a regular shirt—she was always *so cold*— and there were her ribs, misplaced wings broken free. She danced her fingers underneath. There was a diamond dip I could press my thumb inside where her chest gave way to pleats of rib.

"Neat," I said.

She re-zipped herself. I hated her fingers. They'd turned at some point to scales. She told me she was going running. I watched her try to hold her smile down.

"So go running," I said.

I went to my room and parted the curtains.

It was so easy to get into that house. I asked Lily did she need a babysitter, and she tilted her chin and said, How much did I charge an hour? Just like that. I left Amelia lunch in the mornings, and threw it out at night before our parents got home. I told them, Yes, she's eating. She drank pounds in water before stepping on the scale for my mother, and everything was balanced at *fine*. We were taking a homecare approach, I listened to my parents say, over and over, sometimes to no one.

I didn't find out the husband's name right away. He was never there. Every day, I waited for him, or at least her mention of him—that he was the love of her life, maybe something more secret, but all she'd said to me were pleasantries like "Thanks" and "Good morning" and "Have a good night." I mostly didn't even see her. She practiced her cello in the basement, a room without windows.

The way I found out the husband's name, finally, was less exciting than I'd hoped. Lily said to me, "George has been away on business," and I said, "Who?" just to make sure. "George."

She let some seconds go by as she looked at me.

She walked past me, to the front hall closet, and I didn't know if I was supposed to follow her or not. She came back with Max's leash just as I was standing to follow her.

I sat back down.

"You two should get out of the house, go on a walk," she said, almost like a suggestion, except I knew I had to do it.

I nodded, and she called for Max. He stepped carefully down the stairs, as if there were a rod in his spine. There was something more wrong with him than I'd thought, I could see that now that I'd spent time with him. His eyes only seemed to focus, and the smile on his lips wasn't actually a smile, but an accident of facial arrangement.

I squatted down in front of him the way I'd seen mothers sometimes do. Immediately, he reached for my hair and tugged. I'd spent an hour that morning arranging my hair in the perfect messy bun. The point of the bun was for it to look like I hadn't tried, and this required mousse and bobby pins and hanging my head upside down for a while before flipping it over again. Max pulled my hair harder. I bit my lip so as not to hate him. I guided my fingers over his and pulled them out of my hair like a stuck comb. Then I stood so he couldn't reach my hair.

"Max is having a bad day," Lily said, either to me or to Max, I wasn't sure.

"Oh, no," I said, trying and failing to sound dramatic and fun-loving.

"Be good, okay?" Lily said. She cupped Max's head.

Max wiggled away from her hand.

"Here's the child-safety harness," Lily said.

She showed me how to clip the leash to a loop in Max's jeans, and then to wrap it twice around my wrist for a good grip.

"You can take him to the park," she said. "For a few hours?"

I hated it when people didn't give exact measurements for time: a few hours could mean anything. All I knew was she meant more than one. "Like two hours? I said.

She looked at her watch. "Would three hours be too much?"

"Sounds great," I said. She could have told me to do anything, and I would have said it sounded great. I didn't know how we'd pass three hours at the park. The only one nearby didn't even have regular swings, only the buckets. Also, even if Lily spent the entire time I was at her house downstairs, there was always that chance she might come up. At the park, there would be no chance.

I thought Max might refuse to walk, but once I tugged on the leash, he followed me without protest. At the door I turned to say goodbye to Lily, but she was already downstairs, the basement door closed.

I didn't make eye contact with Max because what was the point. I wanted to have called in sick today, if only so Lily would have been forced to speak to me, to sigh into the phone and say, "Oh, Karin, I don't know how we'll manage without you."

I saw Amelia's shadow in the window as we crossed from their lawn onto mine to reach the street. I thought of how long three hours in the park was.

"Hey Max, how about if we skip the park today?" My voice was flat and loud, and it made me afraid of myself.

If Lily were watching at the window, she would have seen and shaken her head. The park, she would tell me. But she was downstairs, and she wasn't watching us from there.

In my house I swung the door shut, hard, because I lived there and could. Amelia didn't come down, so I slammed the door again.

"What's your problem?" she called. Her voice was faint, floating from I couldn't tell where.

"I brought the kid over."

She didn't answer me. It was improbable that she was dead. If she were dead, it would have happened so suddenly that this would be the story I would tell for the rest of my life: "She said 'What's your problem?' and then she died!"

I unclipped Max's leash. He wandered over to the front hall closet. He sat in front of the shoes as if there were something moving for him to watch.

Amelia came down the stairs. She'd taken on a smell I recognized from nursing homes.

"I was supposed to take him to the park," I told her.

"Now you can babysit us both." She smiled with her waxy, bluish lips together.

"We can have lunch," I said to Amelia.

"We could've had lunch, but I already ate," Amelia said. She sat on one of the kitchen chairs, her knees pulled to her chin. The stones of her spine were visible through her sweatshirt. I covered her spine with my hand. It felt like my mother's strand of black pearls, which she wore to dinner parties. It made me dizzy, touching my sister's bones.

I went to the fridge and saw the sandwich I'd made her, the apple and Ensure and energy bar tucked neatly beside it.

"I ate something else," she said, and it made me want to thank her, for pretending, for once, for me.

I washed off the apple and called Max into the kitchen. I'd seen him eat apples before. He held the apple by its stem. I put Amelia's sandwich on a plate. The bread was smashed and soft, and I picked up one half of the sandwich, squeezed it between my fingers.

"I already ate," Amelia said, again. She tapped her fingers over her collarbone. She did this absentmindedly, the way pregnant women reach for their stomachs.

"What did you eat?" I said.

"I had cheesecake," she said. "Coated in chocolate."

Sometimes, if I looked at just at my sister's eyes, I could imagine her as delicate instead of ugly. "Deep-fried in butter cream icing," I said.

We had still had to pass almost two hours with Max.

"He doesn't really talk," Amelia said. She was sitting on the sofa with her head tossed back, her skin only barely protecting the long and lumpy bulge of her throat.

"There's something wrong with him." It felt like heartburn, saying this in front of Max, but I also liked the way it felt. Here I was, a girl with her sister.

Max didn't appear to notice either of us. He walked in slow circles around the kitchen. And then I noticed the dark splotch on his pants. I'd forgotten to take him to the bathroom. I'd forgotten to stand patiently outside, listening to the sound of his pee, and then the flush. Extra air floated in front of my eyes. I thought I might pass out or cry.

I laughed.

I was just his babysitter.

"I bet you have some pants he can change into," I said to Amelia. "I bet you have pants that are too small for him."

Sometimes, when she thought I wasn't watching, I saw Amelia wrap her hand around the string of her bicep, forefinger to thumb.

She folded her arms across her chest. "We could wash his pants."

"You don't even know how to do laundry," I said.

Amelia bent over Max and tried to unzip his pants, but he squirmed away from her. I should have told her that she needed to hold him tightly at the shoulders.

"Max," Amelia said. "Hey, Max." He wouldn't look at her because he wouldn't look at anyone. I didn't go over to help Amelia.

She wrapped one arm around his shoulders as if someone had taught her how. With the other hand, she undid his fly. Her fingers were chapped and torn, but tender in the ways they moved.

I walked over to them and held Max's arms to his sides so my sister could help him step out of his pants, and then his underwear. She tied a towel around his waist. He shimmied out of it almost immediately.

We let him run naked around the house, as if we were parents and this was a decision ours to make. Amelia smoothed the pants over her legs before placing them into the washing machine. I watched her shake detergent into the box in the corner of the washing machine. I'd never done laundry before, and I'd never watched my mother. Amelia was my older sister, and she possessed life skills I didn't yet have. I wanted to take this moment and carry it between my palms like water.

"Do you think you'll have kids?" I asked her.

She thrummed her collarbone. "I haven't had my period since I was younger than you."

I nodded. The washing machine filled with soap. "I probably won't get married."

"Yes, you will." She lowered herself to the floor and sat on her hands.

I lifted my key to Lily's lock, now that three hours were gone, and the door opened for me. Magic, I thought. But it was only a man. George. I'd never seen him this close before, and he looked even better than I'd thought, like some kind of *rapist*. I let the key drop into my pocket.

"The babysitter," he said.

"I'm the babysitter," I echoed, like an immigrant fresh off some boat.

He passed a palm quickly over Max's hair, as if someone had told him to. Max swatted the hand away, and ran down the stairs to the basement, but then he ran up again. And down again.

"Do you need to be taken home?"

I leaned back on the heels of my sneakers.

He shook his head. "How obtuse of me. You live close by; my wife did tell me that."

I let my feet fall forward. "You're not away on business?"

He smiled at me slowly, like I'd asked him what my own name was.

"Business canceled." He smiled again. "So you live right around here?"

I was hurt that he didn't realize I lived across the street from him, that at night, he had never, as I'd hoped he had, watched me. I'd imagined him and Lily peering into my room—my own curtains parted for them—and imagining a daughter, me as their perfect daughter.

It wasn't time for me to leave, and anyway, I didn't want to walk across the street and be home. I wanted him to drive me somewhere far, for us to sit side by side, him asking me questions like what grade was I going into and what was my favorite subject; did I know what I wanted to be when I grew up? I thought of the farthest place from my house I knew the way to.

"I actually need a ride to the hospital," I said. "My sister, you know."

George nodded, but I could tell he didn't know. I wondered what he thought when he saw my sister. Even if he didn't see me, he would have had to see Amelia, jogging around the block, over and over.

"She has cancer," I said. It's not like she has cancer! my mother said once to my father, when I was young enough to think what she meant by this was relief.

George raised his eyebrows and stepped back, as if our fingers had touched in a bolt of static electricity.

Cancer. I held the word on my tongue like melting chocolate. I loved Amelia just then, Amelia with cancer. Now, the dinner table with Amelia slipping food to me beneath the table, my parents watching her, but not me, as I ate, and the nights my father ordered in pizza and ate it alone in front of the TV, the rest of us referring to him distantly, as if he were away on some trip, this could be easily explained: My sister was unfairly stricken, a martyr, weathering the burdens of her illness with uncommon grace. Cancer of the kidneys, I could tell George, because it was true her kidneys was failing, her skin now the understated yellow of diluted urine. Cancer of the liver, the pancreas, the stomach.

"Cancer of the bones," I said.

"So you need a ride?" he asked, as if I'd presented him with a confusing logistical problem.

"I live across the street," I said. "I don't need a ride there."

He squinted at me. "I'll just let Lily know." He and Max took the stairs together, and I wondered if George thought his son was following him on purpose.

I wanted, more than I wanted most things, to go with them down the stairs. I wanted to see Lily at her cello. I wanted to watch her play. No, I wanted her to play for me. I didn't go downstairs, though, because if I did, there would be a family gathered around a cello, and also me, too tall to be a child of theirs.

The basement door opened, and Lily emerged, Max squirming on her hip. He was smiling his sort-of smile. George was behind them, to catch them, I imagined, if Lily fell from Max's weight.

"His business was canceled," Lily said to me. She was looking at George. They were standing close to each other, but not touching.

"Sometime business gets canceled," George said.

"Business—and women—can be so capricious, can't they?" Lily said.

"You need a ride to the hospital?" Lily said to me, still looking at him. She swallowed the way I sometimes saw my mother swallow.

"Because my sister has cancer," I said.

If just Lily, or just George, were driving me, I'd sit in front, next to one of them, and they'd ask me to adjust the radio or the air conditioning. Instead, I had to sit with Max, in the back. Max had a car seat even though he was old for that. Lily asked me to strap him in. I missed the buckle twice, almost gave up, then got it.

I asked Lily and George if they worked together. I was sure they'd tell me, in fact, yes, they did work together, and then tell me how they met.

"No," George said. He asked me for directions, and I told him the regular directions, and the shortcut directions, to show I'd been to the hospital more times than a person whose sister was not often gravely ill.

"I don't suppose you listen to much cello playing, Carol?" he said.

I was embarrassed of the way I must have mumbled when I'd introduced myself. *Carol. Karin.* "I love the cello," I said.

"Do you play?" Lily asked.

The worst possible answer I could give to her question was yes, and when I heard myself say it, I felt as if I were equally capable of jumping in front of a train, or smothering Max, or telling my parents, no, Amelia wasn't eating: all these things I was not supposed to do.

"Well," Lily said. "Maybe you and I could play together sometime."

"That would be really fun," I said. And then I kept talking. "I don't get to play as much as I'd like because my sister's so sick. We had to sell my cello. To pay for treatment."

George looked at me in the rearview mirror. "That's enough," he said, like a father, though not mine.

We pulled up at the hospital, and I started to unbuckle my seatbelt, then stopped. I didn't want to go to the hospital. I didn't want to walk through florescent hallways and see trays of individually packaged sliced bread, cans of Ensure, IVs and blood pressure machines, nurses in cartoon-patterned scrubs, doctors with their lab coats open, and lines of girls, all of whom would not be my sister.

"I forgot," I said. "My sister already died."

"She already died," George repeated.

I knew I should've felt bad about lying, but I felt sort of terrific, because though there were limits involved in being the sister of a sick sister, the possibilities were boundless for sisters of dead sisters, sisters who were forced, in conversation, to say, I don't have a sister.

"I need a dress for the funeral," I said. "Can you take me to buy a dress?"

"Your sister's not dead," George said.

"Ask anybody." My heart banged against my ribcage. "Ask any doctor in the whole hospital. Ask a nurse. Ask the receptionist, or the other patients, or their visitors."

Lily held the head-rest and turned around. "I might have a dress for you," she said. "Black, right?"

"Lily," George said, but at the same time, I said, "Yes."

We pulled into the driveway and Lily reached toward Max, her fingers sweeping his cheeks. "We're home," she said. "You're home." Max didn't answer, and I wondered how it was that Lily continued to talk to him, knowing he'd never say anything back.

George parked the car. He didn't look at any of us, just went inside and shut the door as if we wouldn't be following him within seconds. Lily unstrapped Max, which I should have thought to do. Max tried to bite her wrists, but she pulled them away in time. I would've thought there was a better trick than that. Max smiled his strange smile.

In the house, George was standing at the fridge. He turned around. "Max's dinner?"

"There's a plate. We're doing no wheat now," Lily said.

George nodded. He closed the fridge. Then, shaking his head, he opened it again. He put Max's plate in the microwave. Max began to bang his head against the wall, as if to a beat.

"You need a dress," Lily said, like she was thinking out loud.

I nodded. She turned to me, and for a moment I wondered if I was supposed to hug her, and then that moment passed, and I couldn't believe I'd even had that thought.

"I have dresses." She was talking to me, but looking at George.

George bent over Max's plate and unpeeled the condensation-beaded saran wrap. He sat at the table, next to the plate. Max continued banging his head. He sounded like a healthy heart, the way my own heart sounded in Dr. Feingold's office, the way my sister's heart hadn't in forever.

"That's not fair," George said, though Lily hadn't said anything. He stood, and I thought he would leave the room, the way my father would have if, in our house, something were called unfair. But George went over to his son. He placed both palms over Max's ears. He guided Max away from the wall even as he punched and kicked, his jaw working over air. George sat beside him at the table, the small set of shoulders next to the big set, like a model of what might be.

It turned out Lily did have dresses. She kept them in the basement, as if they went along with the cello.

"These are for my recitals," she said.

I thought of what someone who wasn't me would say in this situation, and I said, "You must play all the time."

She reached for a dress. "This one's black," she said.

They were all black. From a distance, they all looked like the same dress, the color uniform, the length so similar it seemed she'd had them identically hemmed. The sleeves of each were like bat wings. There were details that were different: one dress had, at the collar, a tiny flower; one was velvet, another, silk.

"Have you ever been to a funeral?" I asked her.

She held out a dress, the hanger at her neck, ruffles falling over her knees.

"My sister's not dead," I said, which was not what I meant to say. I meant to comment on the cello, or to tell her she was beautiful, or to ask her about her recitals: when she had started playing, maybe.

"This dress might be a little old for you." Lily nodded, as if I'd been the one to say this, originally, and she still thought my sister was dead.

"Why don't you try this?" She handed me the dress with the tiny flower.

I took the dress from her. I held it against my body and could tell immediately that it would be too small. Amelia could have worn the dress without unzipping it.

"I should try it on now?"

"We're just women here," Lily said.

I'd never been called a woman before, and though I liked the way it sounded, I also knew she was wrong. I took off my shirt, but left my jeans on.

"You can just lift up your arms," Lily told me, and slid the dress over my head, like a mother would.

I looked terrible.

Lily touched the zipper at my back, and I felt a droplet of sweat slip down between my breasts like an awful tear. But she didn't try to zip it. She just kept her hand where it was, on the small of my back. It made me shiver in a good way.

"I wore that to my first recital," she said. "Back before Max, before George. My mother bought me that dress. I loved that dress, and that night, I played better than I'd ever played, you know?"

Now I understood her.

I turned around. "Your mother died?"

Lily smiled a little bit. "My mother still thinks she's too young to be a grandmother," she said.

I didn't have anything to say to that. I wanted Lily to stop talking about her mother. I wanted her to talk about George, and how she was in love with him. Because I saw them, at night, when they thought no one did, and I watched them sleep, and sometimes I watched one or both of them wake, and I knew it was for Max.

"Would you play for me?" I said.

Lily touched the flower at my throat. She brought her fingers to her own throat. "Is there a particular piece?"

I wiped my hands on the dress. In the mirror I watched the way my face didn't change. I looked like a person who never felt anything.

"There isn't a piece," I said.

Lily walked over to the cello. She positioned herself on a chair, the cello between her legs. She lifted the bow. She rested the cello's neck against her shoulder, her fingers winking over the strings like shadow puppets. With her other hand, she moved the bow. Lily's face, as she played, seemed to round out and smoothen, shadows disappearing impossibly beneath her eyes. I saw that she couldn't see me, or the room we were in, or herself. She couldn't hear her husband or her son, right above us. And next door, the house where my family lived, that was another country, but a small one, a place and people she didn't have the time to imagine or wonder about.

SURROGATE

There's never enough work for Sophie, but Professor Schapiro says it's not important that she do something, but that she be. He's paying her cash. Sophie is helping Professor Schapiro with footnotes for a book called, right now, *The Scandal of Hansel and Gretel: Incest and Other Mischief.* All the research is done in his house. His office is in his bedroom. Professor Schapiro asks, a lot of the time, does Sophie hear the internal slant rhyme in "Hansel" and "scandal"? He barely moves when he asks her, as if the fate of the entire book depends on her hearing the rhyme. He's growing a beard, and it's now at the point where it sticks out from the sides of his face like the hands of people shouting, Surprise! Only the beard quivers while he waits for her answer.

He was Sophie's undergrad thesis adviser for her dead-in-the-water English major. Sophie was interested in Virginia Woolf, but Professor Schapiro had looked almost stricken at the suggestion. So she'd written about "The Frog Prince," which he'd liked. Sophie's favorite part of the story was when the princess threw the frog against the wall instead of fucking him. Professor Schapiro likes Sophie for no reason she can see. It's as if he'd glanced up and seen her at exactly the moment he was looking for someone, anyone.

He hadn't been a popular professor; being in his class was like trying to catch a train. Sometimes you got there just in time, and other times you missed it and ending up just waiting and waiting, balancing on the precipice of giving up. And he was a harsh grader, scrawling illegible, unintelligible shorthand all over a paper. Didn't I teach this? he'd plaintively ask the class. Didn't we go over this? But he'd offered to be her advisor, awarded her an uncalled-for A. And he'd given her this gig, paying her too much, explaining she was his first choice.

Doing nothing is more difficult than it would seem, though, and so Sophie creates tasks for herself. She gets coffee. Usually, Mrs. Schapiro, who also works from home, ignores her, but today when Sophie says, mild as cottage cheese, "Professor Schapiro asked for a coffee, do you want one?", Mrs. Schapiro's eyes get very bright and she smiles.

"What do you do when you're with my husband?" she says. "*With* him." She winks extravagantly.

"Mostly nothing," Sophie says. Because, aside from its being true, isn't this what Mrs. Schapiro has been hoping to hear?

But Mrs. Schapiro frowns. She and Professor Schapiro have an open marriage, she explains. Picture, Mrs. Schapiro says, a mouth at the dentist. And now Mrs. Schapiro demonstrates with her own mouth, opening wide enough for Sophie to see the silver inside her molars: ahhhh.

"I, for instance," Mrs. Schapiro continues, "am on the table four days a week with my acupuncturist. *With* him." And here again is the wink.

"I wonder if you'd like to see my office," says Mrs. Schapiro, and begins walking away. She walks quickly, but not so quickly as to suggest she doesn't mean for Sophie to follow her, which Sophie does.

Unlike Professor Schapiro, Mrs. Schapiro has an actual office with a large, antique desk and a window.

"A room of one's own," Sophie says, delighted with herself

for the reference.

But Mrs. Schapiro just looks at her. "My office," she says, very slowly, as though it has occurred to her that Sophie might not be fluent in English after all.

Mrs. Schapiro, it turns out, is much more interested in her own writing than in anyone else's. Mrs. Schapiro is hard at work on a children's book that will, if all goes to plan, become a wildly successful series. The book is about a little girl named Frances. Frances is a puff of yellow for hair on a body made of sticks with a triangle that's a skirt. When she runs, she's all elbows and dust, and the freckles on her nose are actually stars. Once the series launches, each book will begin the same way: "Frances loves living in France. Frances does not have any parents. Her parents are dead as doornails."

The books will help children grapple with their desire to kill their parents, Mrs. Schapiro explains. All children want to kill their parents. "Surely you'd agree?" Mrs. Schapiro asks.

"I guess," says Sophie.

"You shouldn't be doing 'mostly nothing' with my husband," Mrs. Schapiro says, and Sophie is flattered that Mrs. Schapiro has remembered and filed away her comment, even if it was only from a few minutes ago.

Mrs. Schapiro frowns deeply, or seems to. There aren't any lines. "Poor Sophie."

Sophie does sometimes think of herself as poor. Her sadness is like a lapdog, begging to be held, carried close to the heart. The sadness (on insurance forms, it's depression) gets in the way, her therapist says, of the work Sophie must do on herself. Work. As though Sophie is a roof with gutters in need of repair. Part of the work is to set long-term goals, engage more fully in life. Live a little. Her therapist isn't entirely sure of this job—it seems more like treading water, running in place—but her father is pleased. He thinks Sophie's here gaining experience and connections for graduate school. Who wouldn't want to go to graduate school? her father says, and it's not a question.

"We have to fix this," Mrs. Schapiro says. "Every person deserves a life of adventure."

She tells Sophie she would like to enlist her in a project. The trouble, Mrs. Schapiro says, is simple. She needs a child. If she's going to write children's books, but she doesn't have a child, some people might think it doesn't look right. She, a woman without a child, might be frightening, and that might affect her book sales.

"It was different before the Internet became such a thing," says Mrs. Schapiro. "Now everyone's Googling."

She shakes her head like there's water in her ears. "It isn't enough to be infertile these days! Now everyone says, Well, have you thought of this? And, Is this something you've tried? Chinese little girls are harder to get these days. You need those African babies with flies around their heads."

Mrs. Schapiro spreads her arms, fingers splayed. "It's all over the Internet."

And now she lowers her voice to a hoarse whisper even though no one else is there. "Surrogacy is an option."

Sophie understands how bad the idea is, but she'd like to see it gather into itself, watch it hideously bloom. "You want me to carry your baby?"

"We can compensate you," Mrs. Schapiro says, smooth as a stockbroker.

She smiles like someone's behind her, yanking up the strings. "Isn't this material you could use for a college admission essay?"

"I went to college," Sophie says.

"If you insist," says Mrs. Schapiro, and winks one final, valedictory time.

Dr. Altman, Sophie's therapist, has a picture of a frowning Freud on her wall just above the desk she sits behind. There's a tiny rock garden on her desk, and a tiny rake. And, of course, a notepad and a beautiful, heavy-looking pen that must have been a gift. Across from the desk is a leather couch with removable cushions, where Sophie sits. There's an option to lie down, but Sophie sits. Next to the chair is a side table just large enough to hold a box of tissues. Sophie has never used a tissue. Not even when she's had a cold.

Dr. Altman thinks the surrogacy idea is terrible, Sophie can tell, but Dr. Altman won't say it. She just squints at Sophie. She tells Sophie to tell her more. If Dr. Altman liked what she was saying, she wouldn't be squinting. She would be nodding. She would be making eye contact with Sophie, but all the while writing with that beautiful pen. Lately, there's been a lot of squinting.

"I think it could give me some direction," Sophie says. "Direction" is a word Dr. Altman likes. It makes Sophie think of tourists and maps.

"I might get to have a baby shower," Sophie says. "Would you give your daughter a shower if she were a surrogate?"

More squinting.

"I guess it would look weird to the guests. Like, 'I got a gift, now where's the baby?' Right?"

Dr. Altman asks Sophie if she'd like to talk about the attempt.

Sophie would rather not. "I didn't mean it," she says. "I

would have gotten the job done if I really meant it."

Now Dr. Altman nods. Now she's paying attention. This is the conversation she wants to be having. Sophie may even get her to smile.

"It's the dance you enjoy," says Dr. Altman.

And this is an image Sophie can get behind: her and death in a ballroom, doing the foxtrot. Cha-cha-cha.

Sophie had actually kind of liked her time at the mental hospital, even if you weren't supposed to say that. The best part had been the smoke-breaks. She didn't smoke, but the excitement was contagious; before the mental hospital, Sophie hadn't realized how much people liked to smoke. And it was nice to get outside six times a day, to have something so basic become elevated to a reward.

Second best was Kim, who was forever scheduled for ECT, always on the verge of being tied to a table and convulsed, a block of rubber keeping her from choking on her own tongue. For nearly a week, Kim had subverted it. The procedure—that delicate, clinical term—had to be performed on an empty stomach, but each morning, for something like five mornings running, Kim had darted behind the nurses' station and guzzled coffee before they could get to her. No one, she'd said, understood about a coffee addiction. Next to Kim, everyone—Sophie included—was sane.

"A baby is pretty much the opposite of death," Sophie says now. "I think it's the right thing."

Dr. Altman writes something down. "This isn't literature we're discussing," she says.

"So no symbols or themes?" Freud is, after all, presiding above them.

And then Dr. Altman does laugh, eyebrows raised. They're,

the two of them, in on something together. They've disappointed Freud.

But Dr. Altman's recovery is swift. Her smile goes back to wherever it is it usually stays. "Why don't you tell me some more about your work with Professor Schapiro?"

"On *The Scandal of Hansel and Gretel: Incest and other Mischief*?"

Dr. Altman writes something down. "You find the title provocative."

"It's the title," Sophie says. "It's his title."

Sex is a problem for Sophie, Dr. Altman has observed in the past. But not for any reason as exciting as incest. Dr. Altman traces it back to Sophie's adolescence spent in a marriage-less household. Role models, Sophie imagines Dr. Altman writing in her notes. Lack thereof. Sophie doesn't know how Dr. Altman can stand it. If Sophie were a therapist to herself she'd be more bored with her life than she is already.

"Professor Schapiro's thesis is a little out there," she says. "He thinks Hansel and Gretel were kicked out of their house because they were fucking. 'Up to mischief,' Professor Schapiro writes. The witch is society, and she tried to stop them, so they had to kill her. They cooked her and then ate her. Out, Professor Schapiro argues. They took turns eating her out."

Sophie isn't supposed to look at the clock on Dr. Altman's desk. She's meant to be in the moment. As if there's any other place for her to be.

"You're looking at the clock," Dr. Altman says.

There are 20 minutes left of the 45-minute hour.

"You want to be a mother," Dr. Altman says. Here she is again with the pen, gathering speed. "A mother who abandons her child."

She's talking about her favorite story, the one Sophie trotted out like a young show-horse in their first sessions together. The doctors at the mental hospital liked it too. It's the story of Sophie's mother's cancer. Breast. This detail always makes Sophie feel like she's at a deli counter: And make that butterflied, please!

"My mother didn't abandon me," Sophie says. "It wasn't like she up and packed a suitcase."

Dr. Altman's heel peeks out of her sensible (but definitely designer) pump before slipping back in place. "Symbolically," she allows.

Above her, Freud all but smiles, Mona Lisa-style.

Professor Schapiro tells Sophie to just take her time and think about it. "Time is money," he tells her. But when Sophie says, "That's exactly why I have to decide now," he looks confused. "All these years, and I thought that saying meant something else."

Sayings are more like sighs for Professor Schapiro. They don't mean anything in particular. He'll say, It's just water over the bridge; I guess that's killing one bird with two stones; A hand in the bird is worth two in the bush.

But her session with Dr. Altman has solidified it. "I'd do it," she says.

"But will you?"

He isn't being facetious, she sees. He knows the difference between hypothetical and actual. It makes sense. So little of his life seems to live in the actual. His house is overrun with imaginary children.

She tells him she will. Because here it is at last, shy as an estranged friend, waving a tentative hello: life.

The egg (not just yet too old) will come from Mrs. Schapiro, whose uterus, it turns out, is an inhospitable disaster.

Professor Schapiro will supply the sperm. Mrs. Schapiro has suggested Professor Schapiro might be most comfortable—and successful—if he uses pictures of Sophie while he jacks off into his cup. Porn, Mrs. Schapiro believes, is too tacky, too pedestrian, for Professor Schapiro's purposes.

If Sophie wants the money, Mrs. Schapiro explains, she must be willing to be helpful. Mrs. Schapiro has purchased a professional camera for the occasion. The camera was expensive, yes, but money can buy some things. She, Mrs. Schapiro, will be taking the pictures.

Mrs. Schapiro takes Sophie's cheeks in her hands. It feels almost like love, its distant, twice-removed cousin. "There are plenty of other spry uteruses if you disagree with our terms."

Professor Schapiro chuckles, but Sophie can't see his smile. His mouth has been almost entirely displaced by the beard. "Plenty of sea in the fish," he says.

Sophie agrees to both the existence of plenty of others and the terms.

But later, when they are alone in Professor Schapiro's office with only Hansel and Gretel to bear witness, he tells her he's sorry. He didn't mean it. She's the entire sea.

The photo shoot takes place in Mrs. Schapiro's office. Sophie is to strip to entirely naked. There can't be anything, Mrs. Schapiro instructs. Not even jewelry. Not even a ponytail holder. If there's a Band-Aid or anything else, that also must be removed. As must any makeup or nail polish.

Mrs. Schapiro at first mistakes the red worm of scar across Sophie's wrist for a bracelet, but once she examines it more closely, holding Sophie's wrist, running a finger efficiently up and down the scar, she sees it's something that can't be removed and tells Sophie she's ready. She may begin.

Sophie has stood fully naked in front of someone only once before, though not, of course, as naked as this—that time, she kept on a watch, earrings, nail-polish on her toes. The someone was a guy she'd met on a blind date. He'd taken her out for drinks, and during the drinks, she'd said sure, she'd be up to hanging out again, and he'd smiled and said, Really? and she realized, with that Really? that she'd never be able to bring herself see him again. So when he asked her if she wanted to get dessert, she'd said yes. He took her to a cupcake shop, but he didn't order a cupcake; he told her she really needed to try the banana pudding, and she'd said, Sure. The pudding came in a plastic cup with two spoons. He dipped his spoon deep into the pudding, brought the yellow, gelatinous blob to his mouth, moaned. He smiled at her with pudding on his lips. He invited her, after, to his office. It was night, and his office was closed, but he had a key. Did she want to come see his office?

He brought her inside, past the security guards, to his office on the twentieth floor. The view was magnificent, she told him. It was magnificent. He smiled and kissed her. He seemed like someone who'd be happy just kissing. He was happy to have found her, he said. She asked him if he had a condom, and he whispered, shy and grateful as a groom, I do. She took off her clothing. She let him do the bra, but she took care of everything else. She stood naked in front of the magnificent view.

She said, Wouldn't it be kinky if we did it on the desk?

She lay on the desk. Then she lay on the floor. He said, Are you okay? Was that good? And after, he said, Can I walk you home? And he called her the next day and left a message saying how much fun he'd had, and then a few days later he left her another message asking if she was okay, if he'd done something wrong. He asked her, Could they at least talk?

But she was home laughing at him. She was in session with Dr. Altman, saying, God, it was like he was jerking off into that pudding. She was asking, Where are all the normal guys?

This time, with the Schapiros, it's much easier. They're paying her. Everyone is onboard with this being a one-time-only event. She won't even have to touch anyone. And, if all goes to plan, she'll be helping Professor Schapiro do his part to make a life.

Mrs. Schapiro tells Sophie to sit at her, Mrs. Schapiro's, desk. The desk chair is lined in piling polyester.

"Should we put down a paper towel or something?" Sophie asks.

Mrs. Schapiro looks lost. "Of *course* not," she says. Is there something Sophie's not understanding? she wants to know.

Sophie tells her, no, sorry, yes; she gets it.

"Sit at the desk and type on the computer. Type very, very quickly. You should be typing so quickly your breasts move up and down." Mrs. Schapiro reaches over and takes Sophie's breasts in her own hands. She lifts them and lets them drop. Lifts and drops. "You see?" She's surprisingly gentle.

"Yes," Sophie says.

Mrs. Schapiro places a piece of paper in front of her. She is to type, word-for-word, what is hand-written on the page. "Once I include the illustrations, this'll be the book," Mrs. Schapiro says. "Typing is a big help." As if Sophie is not naked, but fully, professionally, clothed, and a secretary.

Sophie types:

Frances is a star. Her French boarding school is putting on a production of Oliver!. Frances is perfect for the main part, as an orphan herself. To become Oliver, she must undergo a transformation. Frances does not mind. She does not mind becoming a boy, if she must. Frances always does what she must. She pulls her hair into a ponytail and lets her drama teacher, the beautiful Madame S., cut it off. The ponytail dances away on streaming legs made of ribbon.

While Sophie types, Mrs. Schapiro takes pictures. The flash makes it hard to focus, but Sophie finds she's enjoying herself. She sits very, very straight. She holds her hands above the keyboard, and each time she types a letter, she makes the movement come from her shoulders, her back, her pelvis, her knees. She feels like a virtuoso pianist selling out a concert hall. (And, yes, Sophie knows Dr. Altman would interject here to point out that Sophie's mother was a pianist before she was a dead mother.) But Sophie can almost hear the rainstorm of applause, and this isn't about her mother. Not everything is about her mother.

Sophie types:

Frances must miss classes when she practices for the play. She misses her classes with Mr. PeeWee, who wears a bowtie to class but forgets to tie his shoes. Mr. PeeWee is sad when Frances misses his class because Frances is very smart. Frances always knows the answer. Sometimes, Frances knows more than Mr. PeeWee knows. Poor Mr. PeeWee. He cries into his beard. Small mice live in there, and they scurry about, trying to avoid the flood.

Mrs. Schapiro puts a hand on Sophie's arm, right next to the scar. "Just a little more," she says. "We're almost finished. Just a few more pictures to help Professor Schapiro."

Sophie types for hours, of Frances who is a smashing success, of Mr. PeeWee who can't do anything right, of the beautiful Madame S., who is always right, who knows exactly how Frances must behave. Sophie types until her fingers ache, until her vagina, against the friction of polyester, burns.

The implantation is a success. "I've put a baby in a womb of its own," Sophie announces to Dr. Altman. It's a joke she's been sitting on. Plus: how's this for a reference Dr. Altman will feel misses the point, will make her tell Sophie, again, that life is not literature?

Dr. Altman's dismay is so obvious it's obscene. All her usual ticks and rituals are gone. Her notepad sits forlorn on her lap. Her eyes, it seems, have forgotten how to squint. Her face softens into a real person's face. She might be anyone, someone Sophie could meet at a party, pass on the street, sit next to at a movie. There's something wonderful about seeing Dr. Altman so stripped of her armor, or her *tools*, as she would say, were she being herself.

"Does your father know about this?" she asks.

Sophie shrugs. "He heard me throwing up. He asked about bulimia."

"He'll find out sometime," Dr. Altman says. "I think we should call him in. I think we should have a family session."

Family sessions had been all the rage in the mental hospital. Family sessions involving only a father and a daughter, though, always felt more pitiful than anything else. Her sisters never came, citing lives. There wound up being too many chairs in the room, like a party with an unrealistic guest list. The therapy room had glass walls, and the only noteworthy one of Sophie and her father's sad-sack family sessions was the one when a post-ETC-zapped Kim—they'd finally gotten her—floating greasily down the hallway, had stopped to press her lips to the glass like a mournful blowfish. Sophie's father had looked at her, panicked. "You don't really need to be here, do you?"

"I don't know that he'd be up for a family session," Sophie says now. "People who are adults get pregnant. It happens."

"You don't want to be doing this," Dr. Altman says. It seems almost as though, if Freud weren't watching, Dr. Altman would get up from her desk and shake her.

There's something to incubating life. It makes Sophie feel as fragile and powerful as she did right after the attempt, when nurses surrounded her and a doctor stitched her skin together like it was only cloth, come undone. But how awful that is has to be for Mrs. Schapiro, who will never love the baby. And for Professor Schapiro, who's only interested in imaginary children who are interested in each other.

"It's done," Sophie says. "You can tell me congratulations now."

She stands and swoons.

Dr. Altman is very quiet and calm, telling her to just lie down now, that's fine, very good, there she goes. She can put her feet up just like that. Dr. Altman puts a hand on Sophie's forehead, on her cheek. She gives her a child's juice box that comes with a straw taped to the side. She puts the straw in for Sophie, though Sophie can do it herself, of course, she's totally fine, that was nothing, she's so embarrassed.

"Why do you have a juice box?" Sophie asks her, once she is up and sipping.

It must be, she imagines, for Dr. Altman's grandchild, the child of her daughter, whose existence and wedding Sophie learned of in one fell swoop when it was announced in the *Times*.

This grandchild must be visiting. The juice, which Sophie has now finished, must have been packed away for this child, for later.

Dr. Altman doesn't answer, but she does sit down beside Sophie. The clock shows they're out of time. Sophie waits for Dr. Altman to say something, stand up, return to herself. When Dr. Altman stands up, Sophie will be able to breathe. When Dr. Altman stands up, Sophie will too, and she'll run out of the office and into the outside air, and breathe. But for now, Dr. Altman doesn't stand up. For now, she sits with Sophie and they abide together, Dr. Altman, Sophie and this newly-forming creature whose heartbeat she has not yet heard.

LITTLE HIPPO

The academics' children are all bizarre. Reading already at four, siblings who say, the one to the other, "Let's do teamwork," and clean up without being asked. They are all dressed in colors that don't match. Elizabeth has moved to town only recently, with her son, Philip, and her husband, Andrew. Philip, her little puppet, immediately doesn't fit in. They are right now at potluck, where the food is five-cheese macaroni and cheese, asparagus fresh from the Farmer's Market. Stews of all sorts. Philip is standing before a family's pet dog (a rescue; a mixed breed). He has pulled down his pants. "I have a tail, too," he says, his button penis on delighted display.

"Philip," Elizabeth says, but she can't keep the laughter from her voice.

Andrew is very disappointed in her, he says, when they're back home. He's the academic. They're living here because of him. She should try harder, he says. She could at least give it a chance. He thinks the people here are quite nice, actually.

Elizabeth's title, while they are here, is "spouse."

It's not as though she does nothing with her time, though. She plays the piano. She reads books. She has Philip.

"Come on," she says. "It was funny."

"It was embarrassing," he says. "Those people are my colleagues."

"Not all of them are your colleagues," Elizabeth says. "Some of them are spouses."

"Terrific," Andrew says. "That's just great. Okay?"

"You used to think I was funny," she says. "You used to think Philip was funny."

"Well, that's not baiting me at all."

He thinks he's being baited? Now Elizabeth can't help herself.

"I guess it really is true," she says, savoring the cliché she's about to lob, "that a leopard never changes—"

"His diaper," Philip finishes.

And Andrew does laugh. They both laugh. They're so ridiculous. What are they doing, fighting? They're on an adventure, the three of them. They're in the middle of nowhere; isn't it romantic.

Elizabeth joins a sewing class. There are only two other people in the class, both women, but the teacher is a man. He has long, elegant hands. Piano hands. Elizabeth asks him if he also knows how to play.

"To play?" he says.

"No, an instrument." Elizabeth plays an imaginary piano and is so embarrassed. She hates it when she acts like this.

"Does a needle count as an instrument?" he says. His smile curls up like an old-fashioned mustache.

She just, she says. She didn't mean.

He puts his hand on her shoulder, and it stays there, heavy as cement. She doesn't need to be so worried, he says.

It's just sewing, he says.

Their task, this first day, is to get to know each other. They sit in a tiny, awkward half-circle. The woman to Elizabeth's right is a nun; the woman to her left has brought her infant in a snuggly. The baby is a little girl, with paper eyelids and small lips that make a heart. The nun's name is Sister Josephine. The woman with the baby is Margret. The baby is Violet.

"How old?" Elizabeth asks.

"Sixty-seven, if I am a day," says Sister Josephine. Her hair is like albino cotton candy, wispy white.

"Fourteen weeks," Margret says.

Sister Josephine chuckles. "Now, we don't see a whole lot of babies over at the nunnery."

"I don't imagine," Margret says. Her nose is elegantly pinched. It's possible she's had some work done.

"I'm out of the nunnery," Sister Josephine says. "There comes a day in every nun's life."

"Does your husband work for the university?" Margret says, smiling at Elizabeth as though she knows her.

"Oh, I don't have a husband," says Elizabeth, and immediately, it might be true. She's a pioneer of a woman, here in this college town, anonymous and alone. "It's just me."

"You work for the university," Margret says. She is smiling and nodding.

"I work in maintenance," Elizabeth says. "Janitorial division," she says.

She knows she's being awful. Sometimes she can help it, but sometimes she just can't.

"Well, isn't that something," says Sister Josephine.

Margret's smile is only vaguely ugly. "There's something for everyone," she says. "Isn't that right? Isn't it, Violet? Oh yes, isn't it?"

It's almost time for Andrew to come home, and Elizabeth

and Philip are playing with Play Dough.

"Is there a right way to play Play Dough?" Philip asks.

He is the most fastidious of anyone she knows. He likes for things to go correctly, and at all costs avoids a mess. So: jelly just in the center of his bread, far from his fingertips. Craft projects that didn't require glue. A carefully thought out request for a birthday cake absent of frosting.

He might have yet-undiagnosed OCD.

Elizabeth says, nope, there's not a right way. He nods. He's waiting for her. She rolls the Play Dough into a snail.

"Do you know snails are slugs inside shells?"

"Stop talking," he says.

He isn't afraid of the things she is. It never crosses his mind to be polite.

He takes the Play Dough delicately between his fingers. "This is a truck," he informs her.

She wants to inhale him. He's her truest soul mate. "Do you remember being born?"

He wipes his hands on her lap.

"You had the longest fingers," she says. "And the softest skin. Your eyes were blue as blue."

"My hair was black as black," he whispers. His shoulders meet his ears. She can remember what it was like to feel this way: as if happiness could kill you.

"Right as right," she says.

He nods.

"But where do babies come *out* from?" he asks.

It's this kind of question that will get him kicked out of nursery school.

Elizabeth knows she isn't doing a very good job. He's not your friend, Andrew often tells her.

It can be so hard to remember. She does think of him as her buddy, her sidekick. Her waltzing partner. She's taught him to bow and hold out his hand. May I have this dance? she's taught him to ask. And then she swoops him up, takes his hand in hers, and dips him, and swirls. On her hip, they're almost the same height.

Andrew's key announces itself in the doorknob. "Rattle, rattle," Elizabeth tells Philip, her eyebrows all the way up. Philip zooms to the door, her little racecar, her gentle monster.

Andrew picks up Philip. "Mister Pip," he says.

Philip is resplendent. His face, up until now, has been a moon, but now it's slipped over with sun. Andrew sets Philip down. Philip wraps himself around Andrew's legs.

Andrew pets Philip's head and slumps into a chair, but with vigor. "My students don't know their asses from their faces," says Andrew. Elizabeth can see this is a line he's held onto all day, like a hamster with cheeks full of hoarded food.

"Surely that's not true," Elizabeth says. "That would be a hard thing to mix up."

She's not sure how it's happened that she's unwilling to give him anything. It's not his fault that he's achieved this moderate success, and she has not. She needs to remember: She reads. She plays the piano. She has Philip. And now sewing.

"That's funny, actually," she says. "I didn't get it at first."

"One kid said he was taking my class because he wanted to take as many psychology classes as he could. Can you imagine? So I said, 'Well, this is Sociology.' And get this, he said, 'That's what I meant. Same difference.' Same difference!" Andrew shakes his head, smiling.

"Stop talking," Philip says, and they do.

Philip now spends his weekends with Andrew. It's just a trial separation, just a some breathing room for them both. She sends Philip with a tiny knapsack on his back, a puff of parachute. In the knapsack is all his stuff: furry pajamas, but not the kinds with feet, his miniature toothbrush and the toothpaste that is vanilla-flavored (he prefers vanilla to chocolate). The spare diaper for sleeping—only for sleeping now. When she hugs him, his body is warm, as though fresh from the dryer.

"I'm going to miss you," she says. "Are you going to miss me?"

He spreads his arms into airplane wings. "This much," he says. But there's already a look in his eyes, as though he's otherwise engaged.

Elizabeth misses him too much. So she invites her youngest sister for a visit. Sophie is also Elizabeth's baby. There are five years between them. Sophie was only eight when their mother died. And she was so cute. She's still so cute.

"I'm thinking about getting an abortion," Sophie says, when she arrives.

Elizabeth didn't know Sophie was pregnant.

Elizabeth takes Sophie's suitcase. Sophie's hair is long now, but when she was little, she had a boy's haircut. Her hair was a feathery cap Elizabeth would ruffle. I'm ruffling your feathers, she used to say.

"Oh, don't have an abortion," Elizabeth says. "That wouldn't be any fun."

She used to sit Sophie down in a rolling chair and pretend it was a baby carriage.

"Did you tell Lucille?" Elizabeth asks.

Lucille is their middle sister. Elizabeth has never had patience for her. She was too skinny as a child; her skin was too oily. She sat alone in the lunchroom at school and Elizabeth hated it that Lucille had to be her sister.

"Lucille thinks it's a good idea," Sophie says. "She had one."

"She did not," Elizabeth says. "She's lying if she told you that."

"You don't know everything," Sophie says.

Elizabeth holds up the suitcase and shakes it, as though it's a present, tightly, mysteriously wrapped. "You have almost nothing in here," she says. "We'll have to take you shopping."

Elizabeth gets some details. Sophie says the impregnator (the father?) is her boyfriend. She likes him okay. She doesn't think she wants to be a mother. Elizabeth can't bear the idea of a little Sophie vacuumed out of her sister.

"I'd raise the baby," Elizabeth says. "You'd have nothing to do with it."

"You don't want to do that," Sophie says.

But Elizabeth does. She really does.

"If it's a girl, we could name her after Mommy."

"You could," Sophie says. "It would be yours."

Their father calls with the real explanation. The baby isn't Sophie's at all. She's carrying it for some couple. She's what they call a surrogate. Their father asks if Elizabeth would please take care of Sophie, who's been having such a hard time of it.

A stolen child. It's exactly Elizabeth's worst fear, come to find her.

Elizabeth tells her father she'll take care of Sophie, of course.

"I guess we won't be naming the baby after Mommy, after all," she says to Sophie, who looks away.

"Lucille did get an abortion," Sophie says. "She told me."

"We need to get you some vitamins," Elizabeth says. "And

some doctor's appointments."

Sophie nods, and it's so close to Philip's little nod. Like she's hearing and not hearing.

"Gosh, you're cute," Elizabeth says.

Sophie peels off a cuticle.

"I bet you're wondering about Andrew," Elizabeth says. "We're just taking some time. It's not something to worry about. Philip is only there every other weekend. Otherwise, he's here."

"Okay," Sophie says. She looks up at the ceiling.

There's nothing for Elizabeth to do but return to her sewing class. She invites Sophie, but Sophie says no thanks. She'll just stay home, she tells Elizabeth. She'll eat pickles and ice cream, like she's supposed to.

Elizabeth laughs. It's a bad joke—Elizabeth thinks it's a joke, anyway—but it's a good sign. She wants to encourage Sophie. Cute little Sophie.

Elizabeth decides she'll sew the baby that's not actually Sophie's baby a blanket. She'll make it yellow, to keep things neutral.

They go around the room and name their projects. "A baby blanket," Elizabeth says.

"How lovely," says Margaret. Baby Violet is asleep in her sling. Elizabeth doesn't understand how Margaret has managed to have some a well-behaved infant. She wonders if there's cough syrup involved.

"I wish the blanket were for me, but I'm barren," Elizabeth says.

She likes this version of herself: a barren, non-married janitor. A woman in possession of a life that's objectively shit from any angle. Classist and sexist—that's what the group of idiots she met at the potluck would say about that thought. Who's to say whose life is shit, they'd say. But they wouldn't say "shit." They'd say, probably, "rife with challenges." Well, let them just lock her up.

Margaret puts her hand to her throat. "You mean you struggle with fertility," she says. "We don't use the word 'barren' anymore."

Elizabeth would love to ask who this "we" is, but she knows, of course.

"They took my uterus out," Elizabeth says. "The whole kit and caboodle."

"You're a cancer survivor," Margaret says.

"Oh, it was preemptive," says Elizabeth. "A just-in-case sort of thing."

Margaret nods, hand still held to her throat. "You have a family history."

Elizabeth isn't sure what's just happened, how it is she's wound up telling this particular truth. "It was a more of a eugenics thing," she says, in love with the rash of horror that's seized Margaret's face.

"Now, we don't see a whole lot of babies in the nunnery," says Sister Josephine.

So it turns out she's definitely insane. It's such a relief to know exactly who people are.

"I take it you're telling a joke?" Margaret says to Elizabeth. "It's very cruel."

Elizabeth nods. "Very," she says.

And then the teacher comes around with his beautiful piano hands, asking does anyone need help.

The sewing teacher reminds Elizabeth of her final piano

teacher before her mother's death. Charles. The memory comes up suddenly and without warning, like a burp that turns out to be vomit to be swallowed: Elizabeth is twelve, meeting Bernadette Peters backstage after *Annie Get Your Gun*. Elizabeth's mother went to conservatory with the pianist in the orchestra, and the pianist, after hugging Elizabeth's mother, brings them right to Bernadette's dressing room. He knocks and calls, "Whenever you're ready, Bernadette." And then there she is: tiny, porcelain-skinned, with hair that looks like it's on fire. She smiles with her lips together, but generously.

She holds out her hand for Elizabeth to shake, and Elizabeth just about collapses. She does not know if she has ever been this happy, this capable of expansion. She feels herself become large. Bernadette's hand in hers is cool and soft, powdery. She must use a special soap.

Elizabeth's mother tells Bernadette and the pianist that today is Elizabeth's birthday. She puts a hand on Elizabeth's shoulder. "Twelve today," she says.

The pianist says, "My goodness, time passes." He says to Bernadette, "The two of us came up together."

"Where do you play?" Bernadette asks Elizabeth's mother.

Elizabeth isn't going to look at her mother. She tells herself, Don't. Don't. She doesn't want to see her mother smile the way she does when people ask her about her music. It looks like just a regular smile, but there's something in it, or near it, that's mean. She feels her mother's hand on her shoulder.

"Right now I'm doing the mom thing," her mother says.

"Hardest job in the world," says the pianist.

"Elizabeth plays the piano," her mother says. Her hand is still on Elizabeth's shoulder.

Elizabeth does play the piano. Every night, she practices

three hours. Her sisters run wild around the house while she does, laughing and yelling and not doing their homework. They watch an incredible amount of TV. They try to distract her, but Elizabeth doesn't let herself get distracted. She just plays.

Bernadette says, "I hope you enjoyed the performance," in a way that means goodbye, and smiles, her lips in a bow. She smiles at everyone, but Elizabeth knows Bernadette's smile is for her. Bernadette steps back into her dressing room, her movements soundless and so, so perfect.

Elizabeth can still smell her perfume even now that she's gone.

The pianist asks Elizabeth's mother if he can take her out to dinner—take them, Elizabeth too, of course—out to dinner. Elizabeth's mother says it can't hurt. She laughs in a way Elizabeth doesn't recognize. It makes Elizabeth feel embarrassed, and guilty for being embarrassed. She kind of wishes Lucille were there. Lucille would know what to say. She'd say, Mommy, what the heck? Take us home already. But Elizabeth is her mother's good daughter. She isn't allowed to say the things Lucille is allowed to say. Lucille is the bad daughter. (Sophie, cute little Sophie, doesn't have to worry about being good or bad. She's just a baby. Even though she's seven.)

The pianist—call him Charles, he tells Elizabeth—takes them out to a fancy Italian restaurant where small, round candles live in glass cups, emitting satisfying heat when Elizabeth touches the glass, just quickly, with her pinky. Elizabeth orders fettuccine Alfredo, which comes dotted with Parmesan cheese and parsley. Ordinarily, Elizabeth will not eat anything with green on it, but tonight she feels sophisticated. She doesn't complain. She wraps the fettuccine around her silver fork.

She listens to her mother tell Charles that they live in New

Jersey. That she is married. That she has three daughters, of whom Elizabeth is the oldest. That she teaches.

Maybe Elizabeth would like to have piano lessons in New York City, Charles says. That way, she can also get in some more Broadway shows. He winks at Elizabeth. She winks back, ruins it.

"No way," Elizabeth's father says, when they return home. "No way am I letting that fag anywhere near my daughter."

Elizabeth has heard the word on TV, but never actually live in her house. She hadn't realized Charles was gay. She's so stupid. She'd thought he used to be her mother's boyfriend. That maybe he was the man who should have been her father.

"She's getting the lessons," her mother says, and that's it. Once a week they go into the City, just the two of them.

And of course, Elizabeth understands now, she was right before about Charles. He might even have been the love of her mother's short, shitty little life. Because just over a year from then, her mother would be dead.

Elizabeth tells the sewing teacher, yes, she does need help, and watches his beautiful fingers as he handles her needle and thread so effortlessly.

Andrew is waiting for her at the house. Philip rushes into her arms for a hug and she breathes in his soft skin like it's air. She's an animal around him. She loves him so much it's all she can do to stop herself from eating him.

"I didn't realize Sophie was here," Andrew says. "She answered the door."

"She's having a hard time of it," Elizabeth says. It takes her a second to realize she's quoting her father.

"She told me she's having a baby that's not her baby?"

"She's not making good choices."

There's also the mental hospital stay they're not talking about. They hold the knowledge of it between them, though, carefully, like a plate of eggs.

"I didn't have any idea," Elizabeth says. "I just invited her, and."

Philip is at her legs like a little cat. He's at both of their legs, wandering between them like they're a jungle created just for him.

"You were lonely," Andrew says.

She's so relieved it almost hurts. "Come home," she says.

Andrew says he knows how hard things can be, with Sophie.

"I'll stay the night," he says.

Sophie isn't having it.

While Elizabeth sets four places for dinner, Sophie sits at the table, berating her. "You said you two were getting divorced," she says. "You're such a stupid hypocrite."

"I thought you liked Andrew," Elizabeth says. "You've always liked Andrew."

"So you'll just stay unhappy? You hate it here. You told me you hated it here."

"You're just in a little hippo mood," Elizabeth says. "It'll pass."

The little hippo mood is a holdover from their childhood. It's what their mother used to say when they threw tantrums that didn't upset her. Elizabeth can remember being so mad, the kind of mad that lived in her whole body, but mostly the stomach, spine and throat, saying, I hate you, Mommy. And her mother laughing, saying, There's that little hippo mood.

"It's not fair that nothing bad ever happens to you," Sophie says.

Elizabeth touches Sophie's hair. It's as soft as Philip's. "It's so hard to be a little hippo."

Elizabeth's father calls her. He just wants to check in, he says. She doesn't need to tell Sophie he's calling. Maybe, actually, it's better if Elizabeth doesn't. But it's important that she get Sophie out of the house, all right?

Elizabeth tells Sophie she's coming to sewing class with her. "It's non-negotiable," she says.

Sophie fills up her cheeks with air, blows out a steady stream. "Fine," she says.

Sophie wears a tight shirt, and it startles Elizabeth, though she knows it shouldn't, to see that her baby sister is showing. She's actually pregnant. Elizabeth is glad, sort of, that the baby isn't Sophie's. The idea of Sophie as someone's mother is too much. Elizabeth a little bit hopes, even though it's terrible, that Sophie never becomes anyone's mother. How else can she stay Elizabeth's baby?

Elizabeth had thought, when Philip was born, that she'd be able to let go of being Sophie's mother. But having Philip only made her Sophie's mother even more. Because the guilt had been impossible. Holding Philip, loving Philip, changing his endless diapers, all made her think of poor, abandoned, motherless baby Sophie. Sometimes she felt—feels— like she hates Sophie. And this only makes Elizabeth love her more. More even, maybe, than she loves Philip, her own, actual child. When he doesn't listen, when he throws himself down on the floor and screams, and won't stop screaming, or vomits in the middle of the night, she feels that hatred turn on him. And then, immediately, bounce back on her.

I love you, I love you, I love you, she tells Philip.

The class is emptier than ever. Sister Josephine seems to have had her fill of sewing, because she isn't there. There's only Margaret, in her usual seat with the perfect Violet.

"My sister," Elizabeth says, touching Sophie's shoulder. "I hope it's okay that I brought her."

"Of course," says the sewing teacher. "The class is open to the community."

He always looks like he's worried about her. Like he thinks she's just on the edge. But it's not true at all. He's mistaken, and it bothers her.

"How nice that you've brought your sister," Margaret says.

Elizabeth can see how Margaret glances at Sophie's belly and then quickly away, calculating. She must think she understands Elizabeth. She's probably revising her opinion from last week, making space for sympathy. Elizabeth, she must think, is a poor, childless woman made to endure the indignity and sorrow of a clearly-younger sister whose fertility cannot be denied. Who's so clearly having a happy life.

"Sophie's a surrogate," Elizabeth says. "Isn't that generous of her?"

When the teacher asks if anyone needs help, Elizabeth's is the first hand raised.

"You have a crush on the teacher," Sophie says, back at home. It's the first thing she's said all evening. She just sat there, the whole class. It was embarrassing, frankly.

"Is that what you think?" Elizabeth says. She laughs.

"I do think that," Sophie says. "That's why I said it."

Her voice is very thin. It always gets this way right before Sophie cries. Elizabeth doesn't want to see her cry. She hates to see Sophie cry.

"I only want you to be happy," Elizabeth says.

"I'm not," says Sophie. "It's not fair."

"I hate to see you sad," Elizabeth says.

"I don't think that's true," says Sophie. "I think you do like it."

"It's the hormones," Elizabeth says. "I got like that too, with Philip."

"That's *you*. You're the one. I feel sorry for *you*."

"There's that little hippo mood," Elizabeth says.

"Shut up," says Sophie. "Shut up, shut up, shut up."

Elizabeth looks up at the ceiling. The ceiling is unevenly painted. It reminds her of whipped frosting. She'll tell this to Philip. We live in a gingerbread house, she'll say.

"Say something," Sophie says.

She steps closer to Elizabeth. They're so close now Elizabeth can feel Sophie's breath against her face. Elizabeth used to have a game called Baby Bird where she'd feed Sophie food from her own mouth. Baby bird, take your worm! They played this game until Elizabeth left for college. Until Sophie was thirteen.

Sophie slaps her. First one cheek, and then the other. "Look at what you're making me do," she says. She punches Elizabeth in the stomach.

And this makes Elizabeth want to punch her back, also in the stomach. Let her miscarry. How about that? Let her go back to the couple who are expecting her to keep their baby safe and tell them sorry, she couldn't do even that.

"Well, I love you," Elizabeth says.

Sophie's so angry now. Angry, she looks exactly like she did when she was a child. A little snorting bull.

"I fucking hate you," Sophie says. She's crying.

Elizabeth isn't crying. "You don't really mean that," she says, and leaves the room.

Elizabeth calls Lucille. They never speak. Lucille just does her own thing. She always has, really. But Elizabeth needs to talk to her. Andrew is no use. He wasn't there, in their house, when they were children together, when they were three sisters, a house full of girls.

"Sophie said you got an abortion?" Elizabeth asks. She has to know.

"Hello yourself," Lucille says.

"The weather's really something here. Is it really something there?" Elizabeth says.

"There you go," says Lucille.

"So?"

"I did, yeah. But a while ago."

"You didn't want to tell me?"

"No, Elizabeth, I didn't want to tell you. Isn't that funny of me?"

"I wouldn't have judged you," Elizabeth says, but of course she's lying, and of course Lucille knows she's lying.

"I didn't want it," says Lucille. "Not everyone wants to be a mother."

"I know that," Elizabeth says.

"Right," Lucille says.

"Lucille," Elizabeth says. Their mother used to, sometimes, call her Lucy-Face, Lucy-Goosey, Lucky-Luce, but Elizabeth never has.

"I'm going to go," Lucille says.

And then she's gone. There's just Elizabeth, holding a phone that's started to beep. Now a woman's voice comes on the line. Please hang up. There appears to be a receiver off the hook. The woman repeats herself until Elizabeth listens to her.

But Lucille is wrong about what Elizabeth knows.

She remembers being in the car with her mother on the way to Charles. They are crossing the bridge into the City, where the sky seems so much wider, where even the buildings sparkle. New Jersey, across the water, is shrunken and stupid, the houses all in rows like obedient, boring children. Later for all that, Elizabeth's mother says. She opens the windows, turns on the radio. She wears sunglasses to drive. Elizabeth wants to say something, but her mother is untouchable in her happiness.

A GIRL OF A CERTAIN AGE

A girl in Yael's office had been killed. It was all over the papers. It was all over the office, too, in whispers and the tsk-ing of tongues, the occasional, theatrical sob. The girl had known her killer. She'd been engaged to him. And he came at her with a knife. It was hard to know if he'd also raped her, because of the fiancé thing. Probably he had. That was how it usually went on TV. His name was Daniel Ethan Schwartzberg. When you killed someone, the newspapers called you by all of your names. He was sick, it turned out—a man didn't do something like that if he were well. But Yael had met him, and he'd seemed fine. Which was what was pretty terrifying. The men Yael herself dated didn't seem fine, but here she was, still alive. Of all things, the girl who'd managed to get engaged was dead. (But she couldn't really be called a girl, could she? Now that she was dead? When you were thirty-one and alive, you got to be a girl. A dead thirty-one-year-old, though: that was a woman.)

What was the message in all this?

She asked her roommate, Sophie, what it was she was supposed to do.

"Nothing," Sophie said. "Nothing, and then maybe a card."

She and Sophie were watching TV. They were always watching TV. As long as it was bad, they were watching it, but mostly they watched *Law and Order: SVU*. There were days when they left the house only to walk the dogs—Sophie's cocker spaniel, Frank Sinatra, and Yael's Yorkie, Barbra Streisand—and maybe pick up some frozen dinners from CVS.

"But can you believe it?" Yael said. "Of all things?"

"At least she got engaged. That's better than us."

It was better. Another terrible thing.

The men Yael and Sophie dated were like action figures. Instead of names, they came with titles: the hipster, the balding Jew, the enormously fat man. They all came from online. Yael went out more than Sophie did, but that was because Yael went out with anyone. So long as there was a pulse, ha ha.

"We should come up with goals," Yael said.

"We really should," said Sophie.

Number one on the list: Find a boyfriend. Sophie already had a wedding guest list prepared. Yael was going to skip having a wedding. This would be her revenge for years of being forced to be a guest at disgustingly lavish, self-congratulatory affairs. When her turn came, she'd get them with her modesty. Oh, the non-guests would say. Yael is so *good*. And they would wince at the memories of their bloated, frilly monster-cruise-ship weddings. She would just show them.

The other goals were boring: Get out more. Right? That was the ticket? Show your face somewhere, and it'll just work out? Do yoga. Eat more kale. Sophie decided she'd start wearing deodorant—but only if it was really necessary. There were chemicals in it that could kill you, she explained, and also she was lazy. Sophie was getting a PhD in literature, so it wasn't like she lived in the real world where people cared how you smelled. Yael was a little jealous of that.

And then they came up with puns involving dogs and *Law and Order: SVU*: petophilia, pawpetrator, ruffhousing, sodogmy, cocanine. Now all they needed was a plot.

They were also collaborating—this was more of a long-term project—on a musical about their lives. The musical also had dogs in it, but instead of sex crimes, there was no sex. The opening number involved the Yael and Sophie composite character waiting by the phone for a date. It was a duet between a single girl and her dog that went, so far: "I am alone in my house and scarf/arf /piz-za./I sit here and chow/ bow-ow./I try to seem aloof/woof/but all I want is a man who's stark/bark/na-ked." Their working title was *A Girl of a Certain Age*.

They were supposed to be writing a musical, but they were watching TV. They were eating French fries. The dogs were getting into everything. The girl on SVU was getting raped in an alleyway.

Yael couldn't stop Googling. Some Googling, obviously, was acceptable, to be expected, part of the job. She worked for an online magazine geared toward Jewish women. Women, in this case, meant mothers. The magazine was called *Modern Mama*. It was supposed to be a Yiddish reference—a *Fiddler on the Roof* kind of mama, but Yael could just bet there were hordes of disappointed porn-seekers visiting the site each day. One day, Yael's own mother liked to say, Yael too would be a woman. (But first a wife!) She just had to keep trying, maybe lower her standards a little, when did she become so picky? Yael wasn't, her mother liked to point out, getting any younger. Her mother, who had abandoned Orthodox Judaism in Yael's youth for this far worse thing: Cultural Judaism. She was just worried, her mother said; she just wanted Yael to be happy; just look at Yael's cousin—now that was a nice life. Yael's cousin, a cool five years younger, had it all: a rabbi husband, a baby, another on the way, and an in-process law degree she wouldn't use.

At *Modern Mama*, Yael wrote articles with titles like "Behind Every Great Man...Stands His Mother"; "Spice up Your Matzo Balls"; "You Call This a Kitchen?!" She wrote an advice column and answered questions about how long was too long when it came to breastfeeding. (The answer: Never! Do it until the bar/bat mitzvah, for all she cared. Do it until the chuppah. Some of the men she dated probably went straight home and suckled at their mothers' teats as soon as she was done with them.) She was working there ironically, she told herself and also anyone who asked what it was that she did. She'd started at the magazine straight out of college, and she found working there was similar to having a heroin addiction; it was a hard thing to come back from.

Also, there was something about the idea of working for gentiles that felt a little unsettling. Gentiles were fine, but there was just something suspect about them, like an off brand of cottage cheese you might as well not try. And some of them didn't get circumcised. Plus—the Holocaust, right? Those were jokes you couldn't make in a gentile place of work. You couldn't even call it that. It would just be called a place of work, period.

But Yael wasn't Googling brisket recipes or fact-checking the dubious gynecological advice she was offering to Concerned in Crown Heights.

She was Googling Daniel Ethan Schwartzberg. The articles were all speculative. She couldn't find any kind of consensus. It was like a Choose Your Own Adventure story, a *Mad Libs* fill-in-the-blank: schizophrenia, sociopathy, a particularly nasty strain of bipolar I. It was unclear, from the articles, whether or not the girl from Yael's office had known about any of this. The articles didn't really talk about her.

Yael had met him just the once. The girl, Libby Silberstein, brought him to *Modern Mama's* Hanukkah party. Yael, for want of an actual date, brought Sophie.

"What are you two, lesbians?" the now-dead girl asked.

She'd been so smug, and now she was dead. It didn't serve her right. Of course not. No one deserved to die, and definitely not the way she had, hacked to death in her own apartment at the hands of her once-gentle fiancé. He had dismembered her. That was a fact omitted from the email HR had sent around.

But he was pleasant at the party; he passed her a plate of latkes, and she had the thought—that girl doesn't deserve him. Libby Silberstein had been something of a cunt. A terrible thing to say, now that she was dead. Now that she was dead, obviously, she was the best person who had ever lived. The world was so achingly lucky to have had her in it; she had touched so many lives; if there were anyone in the running to replace God, you can bet it would be her.

"Not lesbians," Yael said. "Just codependent."

"Not that there'd be anything wrong with that," Libby said, and Yael felt like an asshole for not being a lesbian. She felt like she'd been caught voting Republican, with a secret rifle locker at home.

Sophie, for her part, was blotting out the oil on a latke.

Yael tried now to remember what Daniel Ethan Schwartzberg had said. Had he laughed? Coughed into his fist and looked away? Put his hand on the small of Libby Silberstein's back? Wormed the hand down to her butt? Surely there must have been some sign of what was to come, even if it had seemed hidden at the time. But all she could remember was Libby Silberstein's stupid engagement ring, the way it winked in the light when Libby flipped her glossy, keratin-straightened hair over her shoulder.

The main thing that came out of the party was an idea for a new number in the musical, about pussies. The cat kind, but with the option of a pun to read into. My pussy is alone/by the telephone, that kind of thing. They never got very far with that song, probably because it didn't feature any dogs.

On *Law and Order: SVU*, another girl was getting raped. This time, it was in a college dorm room. She was passed out drunk, and the man who was raping her was blond and handsome; he wore a school ring, and his name was Chad. It was a story ripped from the headlines.

The goals—the showing of their faces, the yoga, in Sophie's case, the deodorant—were hard to keep up. The dog run was probably Yael and Sophie's most social activity. They aimed for once a day. For Frank Sinatra, it was all about the squirrels. He'd sit on the bench watching them like it was TV. Sometimes, he'd try to go after them with a slow lion's prowl, as if that was fooling anyone. The squirrels were jerks, though. They'd dance around the edge of the fence, racing off at the last second, leaving Frank Sinatra to howl out his despair at the futility of it all.

Today was a howling day.

Scarecrow Lady staggered over with a scowl. "Someone," she said to the air above their heads, "needs to get that dog under control."

Like the dates, the people at the dog run also were without real names. Scarecrow Lady was either anorexic or had a syndrome. Whatever it was, she was terrifying, and she never shared her tennis balls. She had elbows pointy enough to take an eye out.

The other regulars were: the weird man; the perfect couple;

George Clooney. The only ones with real names were the dogs. The weird man's dog was Isabella. The perfect couple had Leo—a cocker spaniel who as a puppy had seemed cuter than Frank Sinatra, but now that he was grown, had proven unfortunate. Scarecrow Lady's dogs were Snowflake and Snowball, which was no surprise. Whatever sense of humor or originality she might have had in her life, it was sucked out of her now. That was a woman to avoid becoming. George Clooney's dog was Gatsby, also no surprise: George Clooney was perfect. You didn't even need to look at his left hand to know he was married; Gatsby was a golden retriever. If a man had a golden retriever, you could bet he was married, almost definitely with children. Small dogs on a man meant gay, married, or in a serious relationship. Pitt bulls were what you were going to get if you were looking for a single, straight man. A hipster might have a dog missing a leg or an eye.

The hipster Yael had gone out with had the trifecta: a pit bull without eyes who was also dead. She was the sweetest dog in the world, he told her—she had been, anyway. It made Yael vomit in her mouth even to remember. The guy, more than the dog. He had a garden on his roof, he'd told her. He grew life-affirming plants because the city air was too toxic for vegetables. He was also making a DIY record. Records had a purer sound, he explained. That was a man who wouldn't raise a hand to a woman, right? But that was exactly what everyone would say about him if he did. That was basically every episode of *SVU*. If you were playing a neighbor on *SVU*, that was your line. That was what all the articles were saying about Daniel Ethan Schwartzberg.

Barbra Streisand hopped up on the bench, growling at the other dogs from the safety of her perch. She was neurotic and antisocial. It would be hard for her not to be, with Yael as her main role model. But she would never hurt another dog. She couldn't, was the thing. She was too small.

The setting is a single girl's apartment. She lies on the couch, a small dog at her feet. The glow from the TV illuminates her face. There's a knock at the door. She leaps into a pirouette to answer the door.

It's her date, arriving with slicked-back hair and flowers. "My darling," he says. "I also have chocolate."

There's a waltz.

The girl sings, "He's brought me gifts, kisses/I'll be his Mrs." Instead of a microphone, she sings into a hairbrush. "Here's to life!/I'll be a wife/goodbye to strife."

And then he unhinges her limbs, one by one.

It made no sense.

If anyone was going to kill you, it would be the substitute dog walker. That was a headline that made sense—"Dog Walker of Doom." It was the perfect setup for a killer: keys to an apartment, dogs so domesticated they had winter parkas, guileless girls. Still, Yael and Sophie said sure, thanks, of course when their regular dog walker, Annie, said she'd be going on vacation and was leaving them in the capable hands of Paul.

Annie was something of an artisanal dog walker; she left them progress reports on each dog in separate, labeled notebooks. She was disgustingly professional. The only mistake they'd caught her in, the singular time she'd revealed herself as human, was when she'd accidently left a big straw hat in their apartment. She'd texted: Did I leave a big straw hat in your apartment? It was maddening. Couldn't she at least clog a toilet or something, just once?

Paul's qualifications were both his parents were vets. Why he had the flexibility in his schedule to be a substitute dog walker was not addressed. The two of them, Annie and Paul, hovered in the doorway, crouched to dog level. They looked like they were part of an indie rock group. Even though it was the summer, Annie was wearing ripped tights, boots, and a flowing white dress. He was wearing a T-shirt with a silk-screened slice of pizza on it, a fringed denim vest, and elf shoes.

Because Paul and Annie wouldn't sit at the table and accept tap water in mismatched, chipped mugs like normal guests, Yael and Sophie hovered in the doorway also.

"So, you've walked dogs before?" Yael said.

"My parents are vets," said Paul. "Both of them."

It wasn't an issue to press.

Yael handed over the keys. Sure, stranger, come up to the apartment when I'm not there. Take the dogs, bring them back. Leave the jewelry. I trust you. And the terrible thing was, after everything, she did trust him. Of course he wouldn't kill her. That kind of thing would never happen in real life. Not to her.

"But a little raping, right? That wouldn't be so bad," Sophie said, after Paul and Annie left. "Sometimes a girl just needs to get herself a little raped."

"Girls Just Wanna Get Raped," Yael said. "We should put it in the musical."

Yael rarely pitched article ideas. She took what she got and said, Super! I've always actually wondered about the safety of car seats. Her editor, who liked to call himself her office dad, was chronically disappointed in her. He valued her and her "can-do" attitude, but she seemed unhappy, he told her almost weekly. He wanted her to be happy.

So when she asked him if he might be interested in hearing her pitch, he all but hugged her. One problem he had was getting too close.

Her pitch was a human-interest story on Daniel Ethan Schwartzberg. She would speak to his mother.

Her editor again looked like he might hug her. "Grief is very hard," he said.

He loved her initiative—that was really, really great, and good for her; keep it up—but maybe she should keep thinking. It took some imagination on her part, yes, he understood, because she was still single, so, obviously, childless, but maybe she could call up a married friend, pick her brain a little. See if there were any mommy trends that might interest Yael. Those he would love to hear her pitch.

In the meantime, how about if he called in a grief counselor? How would that sound? He knew someone personally, who was renowned, and a real mensch.

She understood his hesitancy, she said. But—and here she leaned forward, close enough to smell his lox breath, "What would happen if people didn't write about the Holocaust? The deaths of six million. Even with the living testimonies, we have deniers." She looked solemnly at her hands. "My grandmother was in Auschwitz," she lied.

He gave her his blessing.

Finding Daniel Ethan Schwartzberg's mother was nothing. All Yael had to do was Google around until she found out her name, and, bam, there was an address, a phone number, an e-mail, she could take her pick. She chose the address.

She showed up right at Daniel Ethan Schwartzberg's

mother's doorstep like a Mormon. Getting turned away was not a risk she could take. She had to get to the bottom of it, figure out what made him different from everyone else—from all the guys who wouldn't hack you to bits.

The house had a wraparound porch, a mown lawn, a garden out front with burst-open flowers in the bright colors of bridesmaid dresses. There were three cars in the driveway, all sparkling. On *SVU*, this would all add up to: rich, WASP. There wasn't much room for nuance on *SVU*; if you were a Jew on *SVU*, you were a lecherous Hasid with a thick, wrong accent and Shirley Temple side curls.

Yael slammed her knuckles against the door. She liked the sound it made. Much more satisfying than the dainty ringing of a bell.

She was writing an article, she said when the killer's mother answered the door. The tone would be sympathetic. She was from *Modern Mama*. "Libby's—"

"Yes," the killer's mother said. "Of course. Libby's magazine." She looked right into Yael's eyes, said Libby's name like it was ordinary.

"Call me Gloria," she said. She seemed relieved, as if she'd been waiting for Yael to show up. She opened the door all the way and let Yael in.

Everything inside the house was arranged just exactly *so*: a cluster of tasseled throw pillows on the sofa fanned like an open deck of cards; tiny, purposeless vases lining a windowsill. It was like walking into a page in a magazine. It seemed like the kind of house where you wouldn't be allowed to wear shoes, but the killer's mother didn't say anything to Yael, and it wasn't like Yael was going to volunteer to walk around in socks. But she felt a little awful. She knew she was surely tracking dirt into the house.

The killer's mother didn't offer Yael cookies or a drink or anything. She just started talking. She started talking so immediately, so breathlessly, it was impossible to turn on the tape recorder. It would be too awkward.

"I loved Libby. She was like a daughter. And that's rare, to get along so well. He loved her. He's so sorry. You can't imagine. He wants to talk to a reporter, he asked me, he said, 'Mom, I want to talk to a reporter.' To explain his side of the story, how much he loved her."

Yael didn't want to hear that story.

"There's a culture of shame in our country when it comes to mental illness," Yael said, but too quickly. It came out like one word: There's-a-culture-of-shame-in-our-country-when-it-comes-to-mental-illness. It was the kind of awkward exposition that never really worked on *SVU*. "There must have been . . . ?"

"Schizophrenia? That's what I'm reading on the Internet."

"Voices," Yael said. She nodded sagely.

"It wasn't schizophrenia. That's something I would've known about, don't you think? It was something, but I don't know what he was thinking, because it wasn't *him*. *He* doesn't know what he was thinking. That's what he says to me, 'Mom, I don't know what I was thinking.'"

She leaned forward, touched Yael's arm. This move was an old standby of the men she dated. They'd say her name, touch her arm, think that meant they were entitled now to sex.

"Does that make sense?" the killer's mother asked. "Have you ever had a moment, you know, where you just lost it?"

As a child—as a college student, actually, terribly, when physical fighting should've gone the way of Barbies—Yael had come very close to strangling her mother. She couldn't remember what the fight was about, but she did remember how her mother had become bug-eyed, her mouth opening in a little O, the tendons in her neck as delicate as fish bones, as easily crushable. And Yael's hand felt enormous. She'd felt so powerful, she had to stop right then. She had to stop because she'd wanted to continue.

Yael put on her most sympathetic smile. It could also double as a wince. "I'm sure," she said, "there must be people out there who have."

On her way out, she found some neighbors who said just what they should: We would never have imagined! He's the last person we would have thought! They rattled off their lines so well, they might have come from *SVU*—really. She could've sworn she'd heard them before.

Yael wasn't going to write the article. She got as far as the headline—"A Killer in Their Midst" by Yael Berman—and then she couldn't keep going. The TV was on, an *SVU* rerun playing in the background like spa music. Sophie was also working; she was writing a paper called "Who's Afraid of Crying Woolf." Sophie's paper wasn't about Virginia Woolf, Edward Albee, or the Aesop's fable. She just needed to figure that part out, she explained.

Yael thought it best not to touch that.

What they both needed, Yael said, was a break. They'd been working long enough. It was time to focus on the musical. The hacking-to-bits scene, in particular, needed some fleshing out.

Sophie was on board immediately. "It could turn into a duet," she said.

On the TV, a rogue detective was punching a tattooed perp.

"Please don't kill me," the girl would sing. And he'd harmonize with her, "Kill me," there'd be a tender, hopeful twilling of a flute, knife raised sensually to her neck, and then, in a booming baritone: "But that would give me nothing but glee/because I'm cra-zy." There could be a backup chorus: "Hack, hack, hack/Alack." Dancers with hands slicing at their throats, screeching violins, a frenzied ripple of piano.

They gave the killer's mother a few lines of dialogue. She wouldn't be in the room, obviously. But it would be a voice-over, or whatever that was called in a musical. There would be a long silence, long enough for the audience to begin to fidget, and then: "I wouldn't want to blame the victim." (Stage direction: a big sigh.) "They were together a long time. There were signs, of course. But she was a single girl of a certain age."

There. That was a story that made sense. Now all they had to do was throw in a couple of dogs. That was a recipe even the most valium-upped of her *Modern Mama* readers could follow: just add dogs. Sophie had the idea to call the song "The Grim Raper."

ODD GOODS

The chair of the department was dead, and Sophie had been promoted. A couple of semesters of half-hearted toil, and here she was, half-arrived. The deal was she'd stay a full-time faculty member with the reflective salary and title, but take on some of the additional administrative responsibilities that would otherwise fall to the chair. She wasn't the chair, officially, the dean explained. But unofficially, she wasn't *not* the chair. Sophie didn't totally understand it, but the dean assured her everyone was a winner this way. Among her new responsibilities, Sophie now had to read personal statements, and though only a few weeks into the position, she was no longer startled when students cited the school's easiness as their chief reason for desired matriculation. Most everyone who applied was welcomed with open arms. Warm bodies.

The new official chair (he got the money, the title, but none of the responsibilities) was Dr. Sanford Blake. He was Sandy to his friends, he'd told her. She should call him Sandy. And even though it made her giggle—a girl's name!—she did. They hadn't always been friends. Always, before, Sandy had passed his free time with the old department chair, their laughter loud and delighted and private.

Today, in his office, he had an important inquiry for her: why did the female students no longer reveal the points of their nipples under their shirts but dressed instead in concealing layers? Sophie knew what he meant, but pretended not to, so as to seem sophisticated. To edify her, he googled "girls showing nipples" and came up with a dazzling array of images. Sophie tried to stand in a way that made it seem like this was no big deal. Shoulders straight, but not too straight. Like this wasn't thrilling. As though she were not viewing pornography at work.

"Want to hear about my latest conquest?" she asked, and Sandy nodded, like she was interesting.

Last night's date had self-identified as an Artist. She'd found him hunched over a sketchbook when she got to the coffee house (he didn't want, he'd said, to invest in dinner). His neck, bent to draw, was delicate as though carved from soap, and as white. He was drawing his cellphone. "It's objects in their environments I'm really interested in exploring," he told her. "So it's like, a cellphone. On a coffee table." He didn't just do coffee tables, he explained, it could be any environment.

"And any object?" she asked, and he said, "No." Not any object. And he'd looked at her with very narrowed eyes.

Now, Sandy leaned forward so their faces were close to touching. But maybe it was a hearing issue; maybe a hearing aid had never occurred to him. He was close to forty years older than her.

"Just remember," he said, "the odds are good." And then, gesturing toward himself, "But the goods are odd." He looked again at the computer screen, illuminated.

Sophie's elective this semester was focused on fairytales, entitled "The Sound and the Fairy." It didn't succeed in suggesting the meaning of her course, but no one paid attention to course titles. (And titles, it turned out, were all she had to add to the world of lit. crit. Her personal triumph, for a paper that

glancingly mentioned *Don Quixote*, was "Tender is the Knight.")
She was teaching "Donkey Skin," a Cinderella variant in which
the Cinderella character's father decided, after his wife's death,
that his daughter might not be such a bad replacement.

The class objected to the storyline: Why did the story have
to involve incest?

The question flummoxed Sophie. "Why is a door called a
door?" she answered after some thought. Met with blank stares,
she elaborated: "How would I know?"

She figured it was as good a time as any to compare and
contrast. She drew two columns on the blackboard. "Good,"
she wrote, the letters slanting downward, almost off the board.
"Evil."

A student wearing a backward baseball cap—ironically, she
guessed—shook his head in a long-suffering way. He would
explain the world to her. "There really isn't such a thing as good
and bad, because people are multifauceted."

"Multifaceted," Sophie said.

"Multi*fauceted*." The student made a twisting motion with
his wrist for clarity.

Sophie tried again: "What qualities of a fable does the story
have?"

"There was no such thing as a fable back then," the same
student informed her, slouching in his seat, legs planted solidly
apart.

Sophie had imagined teaching would be like an extended
conversation with acquaintances—polite, and without much
obligation, on either party's part, to pay attention. It was not
that.

She sat at her desk, considering her options. "Do you see
anything in my teeth?" she said at last, pulling back her lips.

They stared at her.

She tried again. "I had a poppy seed bagel this morning, so."

"I like those kinds of bagels," offered her best student, Zachary, who could always be counted on to help. He was older than most of the students, a returning student after some years of a probably drug-related sabbatical. He was also married. His wife was a homemaker, caring, sweetly, for their infant twins. Sophie knew this because she'd asked. She wanted to be the kind of teacher who was friends with her students, but so far Zachary was the closest she'd come, and they were not friends.

"I actually like cinnamon raisin better," Sophie continued. "So it's funny."

She felt like she was in a play and had lost her lines.

She went back to comparing and contrasting on the board, but this time she didn't ask for their input. She put everything she could think of on either side of her chart, and then she wrote down the next night's reading. And then she dismissed them early, which the old, dead department chair had warned her against doing. It would amount to a robbery, he'd said. Now that she thought of it, this might actually have been the last thing the old chair had said to her, his dying words of wisdom. She imagined herself with a ski mask and gun: Give me all your education!

"Oh, hey," she said now to Zachary, who was just about to, but had not just yet, left her classroom. He'd just lifted his backpack—she loved that he wore a backpack—onto his shoulders. "Would you mind coming by my office for a minute?"

"Am I in trouble?" he said, and she could have kissed him for how he, so misguidedly, respected her.

She waved at his face. "There's just something I've been meaning to ask you."

Leave your wife! Be my husband! She would refrain from asking that.

Her office was not strictly hers, but one she shared with three other professors. One, Professor Greene, was her frenemy. Professor Greene had perfected the art of the backhanded insult and the seemingly inadvertent self-compliment.

When she'd heard about Sophie's fairy tale elective, for example, she'd closed her eyes meaningfully. "I have an almost-finished dissertation on fairytales and folklore. But I guess they wanted someone good to teach the survey courses. The fundamentals."

She'd opened her eyes, nodding and smiling at Sophie, as if to tell Sophie she was very welcome for hearing her, Professor Greene's, thoughts. Professor Greene spoke often about her almost-finished dissertation, which she hadn't managed to finish just yet, because she'd fallen in love, and now had two genius children, aged six and seven, who were even smarter than Professor Greene's pupils, and who filled her life. Her almost-finished dissertation was kept in a box in Professor Greene's basement (who had room for a dissertation among all the shining pictures of the perfect family?). Rest assured, it was wonderful; Professor Greene had gone to Yale for undergrad, and this made her very smart. The Ivies were selective, Professor Greene explained to Sophie, who had gone to a state school.

The other professors were more benign. Iris, a mother figure and matchmaker who'd been there twenty-two years, had taken Sophie under her wing. She regularly set Sophie up on blind dates—one was due to take place that very evening, in fact. And the third, Adam, was renowned in the school for being its worst teacher. "That guy brings me down," Sandy said, as an excuse for seldom inviting Adam to faculty meetings, publicly claiming always to have forgotten to put a notice in his box. Sandy referred to Adam as "unmarriageable," citing him as proof that Sophie, contrary to her claims, did in fact have standards, in that she was not dating him. Well, he'd never asked.

But for this hour the office was hers.

Sophie sat down at her desk and took a sip of old coffee, before remembering it wasn't hers. The coffee was cold and stale with a layer of skin fogging the top. She would've spat it out if she cared more, but she didn't care more.

Zachary set across from her, twirling his pen between his fingers like a tiny baton.

"How about that class today?" she said. She leaned forward to show him both her cleavage and invitation for collusion.

"Yeah, 'Donkey Skin's' a weird one."

She tried again. She was always trying again. "Have you given any thought to an English major?"

This would make him belong to her for another bunch of semesters at least. And then he would choose her for his Senior Thesis advisor, and they'd spend long hours in her office together, their knees sometimes accidently—and then on-purposely—touching. She would write him a letter of recommendation for graduate school.

"I was thinking more Business," he said. "No offense. I just kind of have this dream of owning a mom and pop kind of store, and living above it, you know? And my kids could man the register sometimes, and grow up with that." He shook his head, smiled. "I guess you didn't need to know all that."

She put her hand on his knee. He looked down at her hand and then at her. She took back her hand.

"I like your class, though," he said. "It's a good class."

What was it that made him so desirable? He had a face she couldn't remember even while looking at him (though she was bad with faces, had once asked a pair of students if they weren't twins, or at least sisters, after mixing them up one time too many. But they were different races, they pointed out). So it must have been the wife. Without her, he'd be irrelevant and unlovable as anyone. But his wedding ring was proof: He was relevant. He was loveable. And damn Sophie for missing that boat.

"Is there anything else?" he said. "Professor?"

She waved again at face. "Oh, call me Sophie."

His ears were too big, pink networks of veins revealing themselves in the florescent office light. It brought to mind deli meat.

"I guess I'd better get to my next class," he said.

"Have a good one," Sophie called, suddenly remembering herself. She stood and opened the door, smiling benevolently at him.

She sat back down at her desk once he was gone. She tapped her fingers along the fake-wood paneling, slick as hair overdosed with gel. It was incredible, how proficient she was at doing nothing. She was beginning to extract an entire intact layer of nail polish from her thumbnail when Professor Greene ambled in to claim the office.

She held a proud pile of papers, marked elaborately in purple ink—she cared about her students' feelings and would not grade them in red. It was fine, Professor Greene said, that Sophie graded hers in red. It was hard for some people to juggle kindness with prudent grading, as she, Professor Greene, was able to do. But then again, she allowed, she was a good teacher with a lot of experience.

Professor Greene dropped her folders on the desk. She squinted at the empty mug, and then at Sophie. "Have you been drinking my coffee?"

Tonight's date ordered chicken fingers for them both. As for dipping sauce, the diner was out. "No *dipping sauce?*" The date made sure to yell. There was not only a language, but also an intelligence barrier between himself and the waiter, he explained to Sophie.

He'd never been on a blind date before, ever ever.

"I pretty much only go on blind dates," she said.

He smiled at her with tight, closed lips.

"You teach, what, fifth grade?"

"College."

He nodded. "It's good that you like it, though."

He leaned forward. "I work at a little bank." A smile, quickly spreading, revealed teeth that failed to go all in the same direction. "Maybe you've heard of it? JP Morgan." And he chuckled into his chest.

She was wearing a gauzy kind of blouse with bell sleeves that swept the table when she reached for her chicken fingers. She was trying out an earthy kind of personality for the date. Tonight she was the kind of girl who had curtains made of hemp and armpits she didn't shave.

"You get out much?" he asked. "Do any karaoke?"

She told him she neither got out much, nor did karaoke. What she liked to do was read.

"Read?" he said. "Who reads?"

"Oh, people," she said, gesturing as if to a crowd.

She was in the middle of a biography about Charles Dodgson and his love for the young Alice Liddell, his *Alice's Adventures in*

Wonderland muse, in preparation for a course she would never teach, a paper she would never write. The course and paper title would be: "Down the Hole: Alice as Phallus?" (Phallus!)

He smiled at her with all his jacked-up teeth. "You've got to get out more." He fired an imaginary gun at her forehead. "Karaoke."

And then he crumbled his napkin in his fist, waving, as if drowning, for the waiter.

Sandy loved this story.

"That's terrific," he said. "That's the tops."

They were in his office (which he shared with no one), the blinds closed and the door locked. He said he was tired of dealing with students and all their neuroses. He moved his head so it was close enough to hers that she wondered if he might kiss her, and, if so, how bad his breath might smell. There was a half-eaten egg salad sandwich trapped in cellophane on his desk.

Sandy was of the opinion that she should call him again, if only for sex. "You know my criteria," he said. "Living or recently dead."

He smiled at her, pleasant as a picnic. "I'd like to see you teach *Lolita* next semester. It seems like your kind of book."

She smiled back at him. She knew immediately what she'd call the class: "Humbert Humbert: Harrumph!"

The college's answer to grade inflation was Humanities Grading Committee, or HGC, as it was pretty much never known. The dean liked it, though. The dean would abbreviate every word on earth if she could, Sophie bet. As far as Sophie could tell, the grading committee was entirely useless, but everyone took it seriously, because it was the only time any of them got to talk to other adults for an extended period of time. The grading committee generally lasted seven hours or so, without breaks for sustenance or air.

On this day, Adam sat next to Sophie, his pelican legs crossed in a clumsy approximation of Zen. He was fighting with Professor Greene over a grade. "A, hands down," he said.

"B-/B" was as high as she'd be willing to go.

They turned to Sophie (Iris wasn't there because, according to her message, she'd fallen, coincidently, on both her wrists). Sophie pretended to think. "B+," she said.

Both of them sat back in their chairs, triumphant, grinning.

Sophie was on her third can of diet coke when Professor Greene's phone rang. My husband, Professor Greene mouthed, each syllable slow and wide as a yawn.

She nodded, nodded, nodded. "Fine, just bring them over," she said.

She turned to Sophie. "My husband, he's a busy trader, he can't watch the kids." She plopped down in her chair, her hand covering her eyes.

"A traitor?" Sophie said, just joking. Just trying to make a joke.

"A *trader.*"

Sophie swallowed some more soda, the fizz tickling her teeth like cavities freshly opened. "Maybe we could call it a day."

"Indeed," Sandy said. He was smiling as if to show he'd been in the doorway a while. He loved Sophie's feud with Professor Green for the obvious fantastic reasons: those involving Jell-O and, sometimes, mud. "I can't leave if you don't leave, and I'm tired; I'll need a nap even to prepare me for the train home."

He tapped the back of Sophie's chair. "How many rooms in your apartment?"

Sophie's smile was sudden as a fart. "Two," she said.

"Excellent. One for me and one for you. I'll need an hour or so to rest up."

Sophie looked around the table, but Professor Greene and Adam both said nothing, a student's blue book spread open before them. Sophie supposed having her boss over for a mid-afternoon nap wasn't actually strange, but regular.

"Sure," she said. She laughed through her nose. "I'll just get my coat."

It was raining, so they split the cost of a cab to her apartment. Her doorman looked from him to her, and did not say anything—he who always told her to take care of herself, dimply supportive as a father. Dimly supportive, to be precise, as her own father, who paid her rent in exchange for weekly phone call assurances that everything was going great. She felt at once betrayed by the doorman and terribly cosmopolitan, a young woman entertaining a white-haired gentleman. Young-ish, anyway.

Sandy didn't mention the dishes piled into a wavering tower in her sink (she'd taken now to eating on plastic, sometimes paper towels if those ran low—but never on the bare table: not that). He only followed her into her bedroom, glancing once at her closet, where her work clothes and date clothes hung beside each other, all her different selves.

He took off his shoes—they were black, not fashionable, sneakers—and lined them up at the foot of her bed. She felt pleasantly like an innkeeper. He waved her out of the room, and she left, shutting the door so quietly behind her, as if happy. They might be married, for all anyone knew. Sandy was already married, of course. And he had children, grandchildren. He was an old man. Though, no: That wasn't nice, anymore, to say. He was an *older* man.

She waited for him on the couch, pretending to read. She jumped when the door creaked open, though of course she knew it was him. It was seeing him that was the trouble. When he was in the bedroom, he was a man in her bed, careful enough to take off his shoes. But in the living room, he was her boss, his balding head splotched with age spots, a skin tag scrunched beneath one eye, its iris the shy, pale blue of his past and gone youth.

"Make me a cup of coffee," he said, and she laughed, because the other option was to feel strange.

"You barely even slept," she called over her shoulder as she filled her kettle. "Are you even rested?"

"I slept for three quarters of an hour," he said, quaintly.

She wished she had an apron. She'd tie it efficiently, once at her neck, once at her waist. She asked if she might give him a cookie, and he declined, and good, because those cookies were past stale.

He put his hand over hers while they waited for the water to be ready. If she didn't look down, she could like the way it felt.

"Tell me about your wife," she said.

He didn't take back his hand. "She teaches at a college better than ours."

"But what's she like?" Now that Sophie was asking, it surprised her she hadn't ever before. It was easy.

"Oh, she's one of us. Likes reading, likes theater, hates student papers."

He turned her hand over and traced her palm with his finger, which was very dry.

She pretended she neither saw nor felt him. "I guess your marriage isn't happy."

He took his hand from hers. "My marriage has gone on for

forty-two years." He would not look at her.

"I just thought," she said.

"Well, stop it," he said. He got up from the table. "You should put pictures on these walls."

He let himself out before it occurred to her she could've asked him to leave.

The dean had requested to see her. The trouble was Sophie's fairy tale course. Its content, the dean specified. Sophie couldn't believe her students had betrayed her. She'd thought their relationship to one another was at least *friendly*. But it had all, apparently, been an elaborate charade; all this time, they'd been scheming against her, noting her every misbehavior, tucking away each for later. She could not, however, deny their allegation: all they ever talked about was incest and gruesome deaths, sometimes Hell.

Now, in her wide-windowed office, the dean shook her head, slowly, from side to side. Sophie knew the appropriate feeling for this situation was fear, but if she were trembling, it was with awe. She loved it: sitting there, across from the dean, her attention undivided, only for Sophie. It was like being in therapy.

"I know our students can be sensitive…"

The dean was waiting for Sophie to fill in the blank with a reasonable explanation, or at least a righteous denial. The college was not one that favored even the slightest of upheavals. It would take undue effort on its part to let go of Sophie, or even to cut her hours. Sophie taught, at this point, five classes at the price of four, aside from her administrative duties.

Sophie smiled without showing her teeth.

The dean pressed two fingers to her temple. "I suppose it's not the worst of offenses."

She nodded, which meant they were done. Sophie stood to go, and a kind of sadness filled her at the prospect of leaving this nice, quiet office, this tightly smiling dean.

"Oh," Sophie said, turning. "I actually wanted to tell you something."

She changed the story, just a little. She made it so it wasn't her apartment, but his office. It wasn't her hand that he held, but her breast. And she had to ask him to stop. She had to ask and ask before he stopped.

There would be legalities involved. Sexual harassment—sexual assault, wasn't it, really?—in the workplace was a delicate issue. Women today, the dean assured Sophie, had more rights than they used to have. Women were believed now more often than they used to be. The dean believed Sophie. Women in the workplace had to stick together. The dean reached across her desk and touched Sophie's hand. A shiver of pleasure ran all the way up to Sophie's shoulder. She was the wronged party, the innocent. She was a victim of sexual harassment in the workplace!

She had not thought of what would happen, inevitably, to Sandy.

She watched him leave for the night, bundled in a parka that might also have suited a little boy, the fringes of his scarf waving like fingers in the wind. He and the old department chair used to walk out together: two suits, two briefcases, a pair of men. But now he was alone, the cold already fogging up his glasses, too wide, always, for his face. He did not look back at her, though she was just behind him.

If he had, though, she knew her explanation would never be one he could understand. He hadn't done anything wrong, exactly, or threatening. And they were friends—or something close to that, now that he was without his real friend, the old chair, who use to advise her on ethics, and who had returned from the summer break with his suits bagging where his body should have been. But Sandy made her feel so afraid. He had taken something from her that she had not meant to give. And (she tried not to think it, but there it was) he also made her feel something else. It was the feeling she got at a rollercoaster's first dip, the horrible and wonderful buzzing on the base of her spine, that smooth, untouched plain where the cheerleaderish among her students stamped themselves as tramps.

ATTACHMENTS

Sophie was getting married with flowers in her hair. She had planned for this, and here it was: Carnations. Perfect. Yael was the maid-of-honor, the best friend. Sophie's father called Yael "my daughter" so many times the photographer got confused, and everyone laughed. Not the daughter! Not the sister! No. But just beautiful, just marvelous, her turn was next; why shouldn't it be? Yael didn't bring her boyfriend to the wedding because he didn't know how to talk to people. Her boyfriend. She called him her boyfriend because he called her his girlfriend. He wasn't really her boyfriend. He was some guy. He was younger than she was. It was fine when people were his age, in the middle of their twenties, and unformed, not really people themselves. But when they were Yael's age it was another thing. If you didn't talk at a party, people wondered: A stroke?

Not really a stroke.

For god's sake, her boyfriend was always telling her, she was only thirty-seven! She was thirty-two, but this wasn't something he always remembered.

One of Sophie's friends from work, Noreen, had sidled up to Yael at the buffet, and was now saying Yael was quite the cougar, wasn't she. Sophie had surely told Noreen this information in confidence, both of their voices low with glee. Yael understood— at a job like Sophie's, at a community college, sometimes you had to be hateful. Sometimes you had to gossip, but it was better to outsource. No use stirring up trouble locally. So no harm done. And anyway, Noreen, if Sophie was to be believed, was an idiot. No one, if Sophie was to be believed, liked Noreen. But Noreen was also thin, pretty, married. She had a child—so how come she was so thin?

Yael said she guessed maybe she was a cougar, wasn't that funny.

"I can't say I don't envy you!" Noreen said. "I'm just boring-boring." She pointed at her perfect, perky breasts, shimmers like trailing stars across the bodice of her otherwise just-black, so simple-I-didn't-try dress. "I can't believe I'm somebody's mom," she told Yael.

She made a face like somebody was torturing her, if being tortured was something that made her also coy and happy. "Do you have children?" Noreen asked, shaking her head to save Yael the trouble.

Yael said no, not at the moment. This was also what she said when the boyfriend's friends asked if she wanted any pot.

"Lucky you!" Noreen said, her voice high with the strain of lying.

She had an improbably earnest husband. "It's so wonderful to meet you," he said, shaking Yael's hand slowly, as if overcome with gladness and awe. And what did she do, he wanted to know.

Yael was a professional stranger. She'd left New York for Madison, a college town where jobs like this were not only possible, but plentiful.

"Madison?" Noreen asked. "The avenue?"

Yael was pretty sure it was an attempt at a joke. Or maybe it was an insult.

Anyway, Yael explained, in Madison, Wisconsin—not at all New York, but yes, New York was of course the best place to be—

she worked for a psychologist who studied infant-attachment issues. The psychologist's name was Ellen, but what she insisted upon was Cricket. It was a WASP thing, as best as Yael could make out. Yael's job was to come into a room after the infant's mother had left. She would walk over to the baby, or not walk over. Smile, or not smile. Yael's ultimate career goal was to get to the bottom of why some men thought it was okay for them to kill their wives, but infant psychology was a start. If you looked at it through the right lens and also maybe squinted.

She switched jobs too often, her own mother thought. Thought and said out loud, often, unprompted. Her mother had liked it better when she was a journalist. ("Journalist" was her mother's word. Yael had been a glorified PR person.) Her mother liked it better when Yael lived in New York. What was so wrong with New York? she was always asking.

"How marvelous," said Noreen's husband now.

Noreen put her hand on her husband's shoulder. "And him?" she said. "He's a house-husband."

Noreen's husband grinned. "She wanted a wife," he said, his hand on his heart like a little boy pledging his allegiance to the country in which he'd been fortunate enough to be born.

"Don't we all?" Noreen said.

And Yael laughed. But she wanted a husband. She would be the wife, chicken and potatoes nestled in her oven, lace satchels of potpourri in the drawers. She herself sagging and sallow and busy, too tired always, resentment husking her voice and elongating her vowels. She'd created this image in her early twenties to frighten herself, but it had turned into something she wanted.

There was dancing, but Yael didn't really dance. She didn't have the boyfriend with whom to dance. The appetizer was beautiful and complicated, little sailboats of lettuce into which bright beads of caviar were stowed, garnished with root vegetables shaved into ribbons. She didn't eat the appetizer, but she did eat the fish, when it came, separating each pink scale, studying the silver underbelly revealed. She was on a diet she'd made up herself. The rules of the game were she could eat anything she wanted so long as it tasted terrible to her.

And then the wedding was over, and even though she hadn't really danced, blisters rose up on the backs of her heels, eager as dogs for her to notice them. Sophie appeared from the throngs who loved her, the flowers still in her hair, the bobby pins holding firm. She smelled of perfume and the sweat that was specifically Sophie's, what Yael thought of as Sophie-sweat. Sophie looked as if happiness were a thing—an expensive cream, a spectacular light— that had been poured into her. "I love you," she told Yael, and she hugged her.

They had always joked they'd grow old together, fill a house with incontinent strays, dogs and cats both.

"I love you more," Yael said.

Sophie smiled, her lace like feathers lifting her as she laughed and moved to kiss her aunt, who was standing next to Yael, and then on to her sister, her other sister, now a friend Yael had never met, lost into all the well-wishers who had come to celebrate how much and how well she had figured out how to be loved.

The boyfriend, Brian, was waiting for Yael when she got back from New York. Madison always looked shrunken after she'd been away, the buildings laughably squat, the sky too close. Brian and Yael were living together, but only because he was, as he put it, between places. The apartment, which was really an attic divided in half, had been advertised as charming. It was the only place that would rent to her because of her dog, Barbra Streisand. In college towns, it turned out, kids routinely left their dogs to die when they graduated, a mess for the landlords. It made Yael cry to think about. She cared about dogs more than she'd ever care about people. All the children around the world starving and left to die, showing up in commercials pleading for her dollar-a-day to keep them alive? Not her problem.

Everything in the apartment, minus the books and clothing, was rented by a company that thought of everything: beds and sofas and tables, obviously, but also a decorative lamp, placemats to set a table for four, fake houseplants. It was a life ordered to go. Most people who used the company were visiting scholars who couldn't be bothered to furnish a home for the months or so they were to be in residence. But Yael wasn't a visiting scholar; she was just a person who needed to furnish her house, but could not think of how. So she was living the life of someone from a catalogue, who dressed in sweaters that came in colors like oatmeal and ash.

Brian was smoking pot from a pipe that looked like it was made of blown-glass, and which Yael sort of wanted to keep on display. She would line it up on a shelf with other blown-glass objects: a small deer, maybe. A little elephant all the way from India. She couldn't even find India on a map.

"How was?" he said. Smoke swept gently from his nostrils.

"The appetizer was nice. I ate the fish."

"Fish *sticks*," he said. "Frozen. Now that's the stuff."

His eyes were so red it looked like he'd been crying.

"Are you sad I didn't take you?" she asked, tender as a mother.

"I'm always sad," he told her.

They hadn't met in a usual way. Cricket's Infant Attachment

Center was in a suite shared by the student health service center. Brian made thrice weekly visits to the center for therapy with a social worker, Melinda, who was on her determined way to becoming a psychoanalyst. Brian's sessions ended when Yael's lunch hour began, so they were always bumping into each other in the hallway. One day he'd asked her how she liked working with Dr. Melinda. (Dr. Melinda was not a doctor; Cricket, who was a doctor, was always fuming on this account.) And Yael told him no, no; she worked down the hall. He nodded a few times. "You should try Dr. Melinda out," he said. And right away she wanted to know him, because he wasn't embarrassed, as she would have been. So they went for lunch, and she paid, because he didn't have any money. "I'm still plugging away at that bachelor's," he explained.

Now Yael ran her fingers through his hair, which he liked because, he said, it made him feel like a cat, and which she liked, because he wasn't balding even at all. "You're not that sad," she told him.

He held a lighter to his pipe. "You undermine me," he said. "Don't undermine me. Sad is sad. Yes, people are starving in Africa. But that has no, no… bearing on it. I have every right, and it's valid, and it's my pain." He took a deep drag of the pipe, perfect as a professional.

Yael told him Africa was a place she had trouble finding on a map. Meanwhile, he was taking a class called The Ontological Problem of Colonization of the Other in the Modern World: An Overview. "You wouldn't believe it," he was always telling her after his class.

He got up now and found a map, unfolded, and pointed. "You are so smart," Yael told him. "So smart and so sad."

He puffed with pride like a pelican, or a little boy.

There was a man, Aaron, who came to the clinic weekly with his little boy. Aaron was a widower, his wife having died in childbirth. Yael hadn't realized that still happened. It was either gruesome or romantic, she couldn't decide. It could also be biblical, which actually was the descriptor best suited to Aaron because of the yarmulke he wore, bobby pins jammed into thinning patches of hair to keep it in place. He was the only father who came to the clinic—disgusting evidence, Cricket liked to point out, of the sexist world in which they lived. Yael thought it made him seem emasculated, and this made her feel guilty, and also attracted to him.

The clinic was just meant for research, repeat visits were just redundancies, but Aaron didn't seem to understand that. It was possible that he really was there to see Dr. Melinda, and had simply gotten confused, knocked on the wrong door. But now that he was there, Cricket said she couldn't in good conscience let him see that lying quack. Why she couldn't refer him to a non-quack therapist was unclear. He was lonely, was Cricket's non-explanation. It was the least they could do. So Cricket gave him a standing appointment and the standard twenty dollars for his participation.

Cricket couldn't quite grasp how much of a Jewish coup this was. Cricket, a WASP, believed cheap Jews existed only in dangerous, outmoded stereotypes. Yael wasn't cheap, she pointed out. In fact, she was quite generous. Yael couldn't bear to tell her that her father was supporting her. The life she'd ordered to go appeared monthly on his credit card bill, along with her groceries and manicures.

"Jews also don't have horns," Cricket told her now. They were waiting for Aaron to arrive, and had circled back to this conversation.

And then, hesitantly, because this was Wisconsin, "Right?"

"Well, you know how the Orthodox men wear yarmulkes and the women wear wigs?" Yael waggled her eyebrows.

Cricket looked briefly horrified, but then recovered. She nodded respectfully.

"I'm joking," Yael said. She wished she didn't have to say it, but she did have to say it. Otherwise, there might be another Holocaust, and this one would be her fault. It wasn't that she believed this, actually, but it also wasn't that she didn't believe it.

Cricket smiled like someone who'd been asked for directions to a place she'd never heard of, in a language she didn't understand.

"It's okay," Yael said. "My boyfriend also doesn't think I'm funny."

Sophie thought she was funny, but Sophie was married now.

Cricket said she had to go prepare some paperwork, leaving Yael to sit alone in the office while she waited for Aaron and his little boy. Aaron arrived exactly on time, as he always did. The only, and so sad, explanation for this was that he came early and waited outside until the minutes perfectly aligned.

Cricket, back from her invented paperwork, took the little boy from Aaron and brought him into the room, sat him alone on a mat with age-appropriate toys that were pretty much the same as dog toys, strewn all around. Cricket left him there, and she and Aaron returned to the office, watching the little boy through a one-way glass window.

And then it was Yael's turn to shine, starring in her role of stranger. They'd been through this so many times, though, that the little boy had come to recognize Yael, rendering the data useless. He lifted his hands to her, and she plucked him up, settling him onto her hip like a final puzzle piece clicking into place. It sometimes seemed to Yael that they were torturing the little boy, and sometimes like she was his mother-for-rent.

"It's funny," Yael said to Aaron, after they'd completed the routine. "It's been all this time, and I don't even know your little boy's name." For confidentiality purposes, Cricket called him Baby Boy B. It hadn't occurred to Yael to ask before, but she'd gotten to the point now, after all these weeks, where she felt like she knew this little boy, and she looked forward to him, the soft underside of his chin, the gummy, dolphin smile.

"Brian," Aaron said.

"Hey, that's my boyfriend's name." And right away she felt she shouldn't have said that.

"Really, it's Baruch. Brian's the legal name. Because it can be hard for people to say the 'ch'. My wife, I mean, she felt like he should have an English name. So people could say it. But we—I—he's really Baruch."

Yael nodded.

"I say this only because, it's not that I mean to be presumptuous, but your name-tag…"

"Pretty Jewy, I know," she said.

"It's a wonderful name," he said. "Do you know what it means?"

And then, instead of saying of course she knew what it meant, that she'd been raised Orthodox until she was eight, that her father was still Orthodox, that she had five half-siblings, all the boys in yarmulkes, the girls in skirts, a bewigged stepmother, she said, "Nope. My parents just liked it, I guess."

She always did this. She didn't mean to, but whenever someone—a man, let's be honest—wanted to explain something to her, she let him. It felt easier. It kept a conversation going.

He explained that Yael, from the Book of Judges (she knew

it was called the Navi), was actually a very powerful woman, that women in the Torah—the bible, he clarified—were actually very powerful, not subjugated at all, that was a misperception. She had defeated a terrible army general to help save the Jewish people. (This, of course, was the plot of every Jewish story, which had made memorization for tests very easy, back in the day.) Aaron neglected to mention that the biblical Yael had done this by seducing the king and then ramming a stake through his skull, his brains presumably splattering against the walls of her desert tent.

"Wow," she said. "I never heard that before."

"I wouldn't mean to presume," he said. "But if you'd like, I can teach you. If you'd like to know more, I mean."

"We'd have to start all the way at the beginning," she said, for no reason she could understand.

They met in her apartment. Brian was a little jealous when she informed him of the plan, twenty minutes before Aaron was scheduled to arrive.

"I mean, who is this guy?" he said. It was a line he must have heard on TV and was now trying out, a tentative flexing of an only recently discovered muscle.

"It's not like we're exclusive," Yael said.

"We live together," he said.

"You were in between places," she said. "Right?"

He shrugged.

"Do you want to start paying rent?"

"Fine," he said. "Okay."

"To the rent?"

"He can come over. That's fine."

"Oh, good," she said. "That's very grown-up of you. And he

has a baby. Maybe you could watch the baby?"

"I'm high," he pointed out. "If you could have just told me a little sooner, I mean."

"I know," she said. "It's hard being you, right?"

"It is hard," he said. "Dr. Melinda—"

"I need to close up all the outlets," she said. "And I think you should go to your room."

"Our room," he said.

What was wrong with her? "Our room," she said. "Sorry. And bring Barbra Streisand. Jews are afraid of dogs."

"Aren't you a Jew?" he said.

He seemed legitimately confused, as though maybe all this time he'd misunderstood and she, of the curly hair and Hebraic name, was actually Catholic. She didn't understand how someone who was technically an adult could be so stupid.

"Some Jews," she said. All right? *Some* Jews are afraid of dogs."

She picked up Barbra Streisand, held her on her hip, where she fit so nicely. She let Barbra Streisand lick inside her nostril. It was disgusting, but not really that disgusting. Or not more disgusting than anything else. "Be good," she said.

"I will," Brian said, and she couldn't bear to tell him she'd meant the dog.

The doorbell rang exactly as the minute hand on her watch inched onto the six and it became 5:30. On the dot. She finally understood the expression.

Aaron brought a Hebrew workbook. No wine or anything, just the workbook. Which was fine. She had the boyfriend. The desk was in her bedroom, she explained, and that was where the boyfriend also was, so they'd have to work at the kitchen table. Was that okay?

"Of course," he said. "It's good your boyfriend's here. Otherwise, it really wouldn't be so proper for me to be here, and then I'd ask if we could keep the door open. It's a law, actually. A man can't be alone with a woman who's not his wife. It's for the woman, the law. It's so a woman should be safe."

Yael understood how hard it was to talk about Jewish law, especially if you were a man, without apologizing. What he'd neglected to mention was that a woman who was not a man's wife included his own siblings and, according to most rabbis, adopted children.

"We'll start at the beginning," he said.

"A very good place to start," she sang.

"What?"

"When you read you begin with A, B, C."

He looked around, as if to find the answer in the floating dust particles she really should have done a better job getting rid of.

Now she was getting nervous. "When you sing, you begin with Do, Re, Mi?"

Nothing.

"*The Sound of Music*," she said. "Never mind."

"Oh," he said. "I'm familiar, but Jewish, Orthodox, I mean, Orthodox men refrain from hearing women singing."

He kept speaking, explaining the origin of the law, its attendant disputes, but Yael was tired of listening. She knew all about this law. It made it so Yael and her mother always went to musicals alone when she was a kid, her father left at home. The idea was men might get too attracted to the women singing—and what? Leap onto the stage and rape them? Yael and her mother used to come home and sing all the lyrics at the top of their lungs. Yael's father was allowed to hear them sing, because the law allowed him to find his wife attractive and it assumed the best when it came to father-daughter incest. After her parents' divorce, Yael and her mother still went to musicals, but never with the same amount of glee. They retired to their separate showers to sing.

"That's so interesting," she said.

"It might seem a little misogynistic, at first, but you understand, it's really about respecting women."

"How nice," she said.

"And that's what Orthodox Judaism is all about."

"Where's Baruch?" she said.

He looked surprised. "You're very good with the 'ch' sound."

She shrugged in a way she hoped came off as modest. "I guess I'm a quick-study. But it's hit or miss, really."

Aaron nodded. "You'll get better."

"And the baby's…?"

"I got a sitter."

"Good," she said. It wouldn't be nice to tell him she was disappointed. It wasn't especially normal to be disappointed.

He opened the book. "Now, with Hebrew, it's a little different, because it's left to right."

They went through some letters and sounds, Yael making sure to stumble often, to sigh and rake back her hair with her hand, gamely laughing at her mistakes, ever-ready to give it another try.

He kept her at it for an hour, and then he told her she was doing very well for a beginner and closed the book. She asked him if he wanted water—was water kosher?—and he gave her a look that let her know she'd gone too far. "Joking!" she said.

He said yes, but in a plastic cup, please. She gave him the water. He cleared his throat. "I'm just going to recite the blessing now."

Yael nodded with her lips together, eyes open wide. It was Cricket's nod, meant to convey polite respect, but only thinly coating a feeling of vast superiority. To the uninitiated, it might appear to be a look of simple, unadulterated terror.

"So what brought you to Wisconsin?" Yael said, once he'd finished the routine and taken a theatrically loud gulp of water. "Not a lot of Jews here, right?"

Now he became excited, standing up, swaying a little from side to side, as though in prayer. The word for what he was doing existed only in Yiddish. He was *shuckling*. He clapped his hands together. "That's why I'm here. Have you heard of Chabad?"

His job, he explained, was to build Jewish community. For all Jews. Even for Jews who were unaffiliated, like her. *Especially* for Jews like her, even.

He invited her for a Shabbat dinner. He said Shabbat, with a hard "t", carefully, for her benefit. In real life, she knew, he pronounced it Shabbos, with a snake hiss of an "s". She'd grown up with Shabbos, disdainful of the less-real Modern Orthodox Jews who insisted on the "t". Had she remained Orthodox, she would have had a *Bas* Mitzvah, and at twelve, instead of the Bat Mitzvah her mother threw for her at thirteen.

"I'd love to," she said. "That's the one with the Hallah bread, right?"

"*Ch*allah," he said, gently. "But yes, that's exactly it. See? You know more than you think."

One thing Yael was excellent at was making herself blush on cue.

After Aaron was gone, Brian came out of the room, Barbra Streisand rushing ahead, barking, triple-axeling with joy at her and Yael's reunion.

"I thought you knew all that," Brian said.

"I do," she said. "That was really weird of me."

"It's okay," he said. "Do you want me to order dinner?"

"Are you still high?"

He told her he was, a little.

"Then order a lot," she said.

Yael's mother called. This happened every day, dysfunctionally and best not ever admitted to Cricket. Cricket, with her cardigans and pearls, probably only spoke to her own mother on a biannual basis, in a country club, the two of them laughing lightly over Jell-O molds. For Yael, though, speaking to her mother was like turning off the lights before going to bed—it was just something you did. It would be hard to fall asleep if you didn't.

Her mother wanted to know how things were.

"Things" took on various meanings, depending on the phone call. It could mean dating a man who wasn't Brian, getting a job that wasn't the one she had with Cricket, moving to a place that wasn't Wisconsin, which could be New York, Boston, D.C., Yael's pick.

"Things are fine," Yael said. "Although…" She waited a drumroll of a few beats, and then, with a delicious flourish, "I met a Chabadnik."

"Huh," her mother said.

"He's cute, also. Even with the beard. Actually, especially with the beard."

"So this is instead of that boy?"

For a moment, Yael thought her mother might be talking about the baby.

"Brian," Yael said. "You know what his name is. And he's not a boy." Though she couldn't quite bring herself to say he was a man.

"You're not still living together, are you?"

"We are still living together. But now I also have the Chabadnik. He's been teaching me quite a bit."

"Is that right?" her mother said.

"Mmm-hmm. Quite a bit about my heritage. It's more beautiful than I ever even imagined. And he's graciously invited me to his home so that I might experience Shabbos."

"He has a wife, I imagine."

"The wife's dead," Yael said. She wasn't going to mention the baby.

"Huh. What does your boy have to say about that?"

"My *Brian* doesn't even know I'm going."

Yael imagined herself as a sexy double-agent: woman with child-boyfriend by day, woman with widower and his child by night. The image that summoned, though, wasn't actually at all sexy. She gave her fantasy self a dash of red lipstick and a trench coat. Better.

Yael's mother sighed theatrically. "I just wish you would find someone nice," she said. "Just someone who isn't a goy and isn't a rabbi."

"A girl, a goy, and a rabbi. That sounds like a good setup for a joke," Yael said.

"Keep it as a joke," her mother said. "You don't have to ruin your whole life just to show how much you hate me."

"That's not that funny."

"I just love you," her mother said. "When did that become a crime?"

It was about time to hang up. A few more minutes of this, and Yael would lose her self entirely. Her mother was a magician in this way. She could saw Yael right in half.

"It's not a crime," Yael said. "Thank you for caring."

"I just love you," her mother said.

"Love you, too," Yael said. They hung up, and Yael had her
self again. There it was, that thing Aaron would call the soul: on
the verge of flickering out, but there.

Shabbos began at sundown, 7:29 this week because it was
summer, so it was odd that Aaron's invitation called for her to
arrive at 12. It made sense when she got there. There was a vat of
risen dough on the table, packets of chicken breasts defrosting
on the counter, a loaf of gefilte fish wrapped in wax paper,
the bare bones of what would surely turn out to be a noodle
kugel. A stack of foil pans. Baruch was napping in a playpen
set up in the middle of the living room, sleeping with his little
diapered butt in the air, his curls damp with the ferocious sweat
of baby dreaming. She kept herself from scooping him up. But
she imagined the heft of him in her arms, his hot body to her
chest, those damp curls pressed against her cheek, lips pursing in
bleary search of a bottle.

"We're the only ones here," Aaron said, in lieu of hello. "So
we'll have to keep the door open."

Yael politely pretended the subtext was not, Lest I rape you.
"Sure," she said.

"I wondered if you might want to help," Aaron said.

Of course he did.

But she felt sorry for him, standing there in his apron, his
oven beeping. "That sounds like a treat," she said. "I've never
helped with a Shabbat meal before."

"Good, good," he said. "It's really not that difficult, once you
get the hang of it. We'll just, we can just start with braiding the
challah."

He showed her how to grab the dough, plop it onto a

floured baking pan, separate it into three strands, bring those strands together. He was sloppy, but trying. She wondered who had helped him before her.

"It must be hard," she said.

He stroked the stubble at the sides of his cheeks. "The Torah says, 'Man is not meant to be alone.'"

But she could see that he might want to say something else, that beneath the quote, which she recognized immediately as belonging to Genesis, he might be saying, It is hard. I feel so alone. My wife is dead and I have to raise this child by myself, and I don't think I can.

She brushed her braided challah with egg yolk. Maybe she could marry him. She could call up Sophie and say, Guess what?

All she needed him to say was, I was so worried about my son, and I met you, and I wanted so badly for him to be around you. I wanted for you not to be a stranger to him.

She would help him: "Most people don't visit the Infant Attachment Center every week."

"Oh?"

Maybe just a small acknowledgment, for now. That would be enough. Just a thank you.

"Because the point of the study is for the infant to come in contact with a stranger. The baby, in Baruch's case." The ten-month-old, she didn't say.

"I didn't realize," he said. "I had no idea."

It was in all their promotional material.

"That's so funny," she said. "Because I think you signed a waiver."

Even a gesture would be enough. A rueful smile. A softly-spreading blush, beginning at the neck, brightening the ears.

"Waivers," he said. He said it the way her father said, Global warming. Nonsense peddled by the goyim and self-hating liberal Jews, but certainly not actually applicable to him.

Aaron looked deeply into space, addressing an imaginary congregation.

"We braid a challah to symbolize our observance of Shabbos," he said. "It's the woman's job, generally speaking, because the kitchen is her domain."

Now he looked a little panicked, diving into the old apology, transforming into every rabbi she'd ever met: "But it's not to say. It's, what it is is the same way that a man's domain is studying Torah. It's not like in the secular world. Women are so much closer to God. Each job is equally important. The woman's role, really, it's more important."

He would give her nothing.

So this was who he was. There was a kind of a pleasure in understanding this, like coming across some old clothing you could box up and definitely throw away, no question. A relief. She wasn't going to marry him, become a mother to his child, save him, piss her mother off, delight her father. She could just keep on being herself: shitty girlfriend, terrific mother to a dog.

But she did stay with him and help until all the challah was braided, each chicken cutlet braised, the kugel assembled and lovingly baked, cinnamon-specked. She slipped so easily into the role of Orthodox housewife, like some kind of inherited muscle memory. Yael could see how satisfying it was, knowing exactly who it was you were supposed to be and then going right on and becoming that person, the *ding ding ding* of a row of cherries in a slot machine sliding perfectly into place. And she thought of her mother, who on this Friday night would set her small table for one, the sitcom laugh track in the background coming close enough to company.

WIFE

So he was cheating on her. Karin found them—her husband and Cynthia Lawless—kissing on the street outside her husband's publishing house, in the shade of some hideous scaffolding. Karin had not been coming to surprise Henry like a devoted, dumb wife from the 1950s. She had been coming to meet him for dinner reservations he'd made. Everything was about the kids these days, he'd said. Let's take some time for us. And she arranged a babysitter, and pumped for the baby (though maybe, suggested her husband, always the joker, he was getting a little long in the tooth for all that), and put on lipstick.

Cynthia Lawless. Her name was a built-in pun, or maybe it was the punch line.

Henry was Cynthia Lawless' editor. Or, as Cynthia Lawless put it, she was his writer. Cynthia Lawless was gaunt and childless, and wore little black dresses that were still too big. She wrote exclusively about sex. The plot: A young girl discovers her sexuality. She's young and afraid and has certain physical flaws like, in the latest novel, bad hair, and she cares about it, but no one else does. That was what the latest novel was called: *Bad Hair*. It was supposed to make you think, Bad girl.

Cynthia Lawless was herself married. If a woman was married eleven years and had no children, it meant one of two things: she was infertile or a bitch. Karin thought bitch. Women in Cynthia Lawless' novels never thought of children. They were in their thirties, forties, and children were never around. Not even the minor characters had, or wanted, or even spoke of not wanting, children. It was like science fiction. Cynthia Lawless' husband was also a writer. A stand-up guy, Henry said. He also liked to write about sex. His plot: a man who doesn't seem sexy turns out to be sexy. His last novel was called *Meow*. In the novel, the non-sexy, but actually-sexy man was a cat. It really was science fiction.

Karin was a few minutes early. Maybe if she'd been on time, she would have missed it. It wasn't her fault, but it was a little bit her fault—that's what she would have thought that if she were a wife from the 1950s and not a woman with a doctorate who'd just that afternoon lectured about Ophelia from *Hamlet*. Ophelia was not a zero, even though her name began with O, she told her students. The O was her open vagina. The O was for orgasm. So what about that? She could speak about sex just like Cynthia Lawless and Cynthia Lawless' husband. She could speak circles around them, pun *intended*.

She should have walked right up to them. She should have slapped him. She should have slapped Cynthia Lawless right across the face. But instead, she hid and waited, and then, when there was no more chance of catching them in the act, when they had pulled apart and were standing at a respectable distance from one another, only then, as casual as a wife who wasn't being cheated on, did she walk up to them and say, "Cynthia, how good to see you."

There wasn't lipstick on Henry's face, because Cynthia Lawless didn't wear lipstick. She was too evolved for makeup. She was fine with looking gaunt and pale and Victorian, swimming in those black dresses from thrift shops that, for all Karin knew, still smelled of must if you got up close.

Cynthia Lawless said, "The natives must be restless these days."

She meant, of course, the children. The children were theirs—Henry's and Karin's—but they really belonged to Karin. She was the mother. But it wasn't the 1950s. She didn't sit at home with puffed ankles and bare, calloused feet lined with just-about-bursting veins. She made more than Henry did. Though that was saying pretty much nothing.

Henry pretended to misunderstand on her behalf. "The end of the semester is always a thing to behold. You should hear the horror stories."

Cynthia Lawless squinted, as though there were sun, seeping impossibly into the scaffolding.

"My students are ready for the summer," Karin said. She couldn't think of anything else, so she added, "The girls' skirts are very short."

And this, of course, was the worst thing she might have said, because it clearly pleased Cynthia Lawless to think of young girls in very short skirts as the days lengthened and the sun's heat became oppressive. It might have turned Henry on, for all Karin knew. There was quite a bit, it seemed, she didn't know.

"I have a great deal of respect for you for teaching," said Cynthia Lawless. "It's a noble profession. One of the oldest."

"You're thinking of prostitutes," Karin said.

Henry put his hand on her shoulder. The hand felt the same as it always had. But the body's memory wasn't one to be trusted.

"That's why they call her Doctor," he said.

"Stat," said Cynthia Lawless. It was supposed to be a joke, Karin could tell. It was, actually, Henry's joke. He would say, Dr. Miller, we need a doctor of philosophy, stat, and she would say, Get a life, and he would say, You're looking at it. It appeared he had told this joke, which was mostly at her expense, to Cynthia Lawless.

Henry didn't catch her eye. He just stood there, smiling, as if Cynthia Lawless hadn't revealed something private. Karin could imagine them in bed, Henry saying to Cynthia Lawless, who was smoking a slightly-smashed cigarette, "My wife and I have this joke." And Cynthia listening. Smoking her cigarette and listening, blowing smoke out her nostrils like a damaged little dragon.

"What a funny joke," Karin said. She looked at Henry, who wouldn't catch her eye.

Karin gave the children their baths, the three together in the tub she really should take a picture, next time—and while she did, she composed an email to Cynthia Lawless' husband in her mind. Dear Frank, she'd write. Our spouses, it seems, are fucking. But she didn't have proof they were fucking, actually. So: our spouses are kissing. Kissing! It sounded ridiculous, gossip of the sort her high school students might savor and pass along, lighting up their devices, their—what would it be?—their platforms with the news. High drama indeed. But here she was, very much an adult, suds up to her elbows, arguing with, begging, her child. Please let me pour water over your head. It's not that bad. I promise. You can't go on forever with shampoo in your hair—you realize this, don't you? Her son, the oldest, who should be more mature, able to handle, for god's sake, a bath, was crying. "I don't care," he said. "The shampoo can stay." He had the longest lashes, and tears glinted, caught among them. Her daughter, slick and slippery beside him, shouted, "I can't hear you! My ears are underwater! I can't hear!" Shouting and giggling, kicking her feet, just missing the proud snail of her brother's penis. And the baby crying now.

Karin sent the email. I saw them kissing, she wrote. I thought you might like to know.

He wrote back almost immediately: Thanks. I'll be talking to Cynthia tonight. Hope things work out okay for you.

That was it. As if it were a minor inconvenience. As if he were sorry, but not for himself.

She wrote back: Do you think you and I could maybe meet to discuss? NP, he replied, like a kid. No problem.

They met at a diner where Frank said he liked to write. The diner served the best French fries, he told her. He also warned her that he took his French fries the European way, which entailed mayonnaise.

She tried to smile.

"It sucks, the situation," he said.

She agreed. But she seemed to have run out of steam. It happened all at once: poof. "We have three kids," she said.

"You can't divorce kids," said Frank.

Divorce hadn't even occurred to her. But now here it was, some grand ship tied to a dock, waiting for her to board. "Have you ever thought about divorce?" she said.

"I think she has the right to explore," Frank said. "I have a girlfriend myself."

Frank's girlfriend was named Gina, he told Karin. She was one of his students at the college where he taught night classes.

"Does Cynthia know?" she asked.

He ran a French fry through a blob of mayonnaise.

"It's not something that's come up," he said.

"You'll tell her?" Karin had tried for casual, but there it was, shrill as a whistle.

He asked her if she was familiar with Nabokov. "Humbert Humbert. Would you just write him off as a pedophile?"

He had won an argument, but she wasn't sure which one.

She kept her face empty. "How young is your Gina?"

"She's thirty-two." He waved his hands. "I meant just as a topic change."

"I wouldn't want him for a babysitter," she said. And then, ruining it even more: "For my children, I mean."

"That's tonight's lecture," he said. "If they come to school at night, you've got to make it worth it."

"But will you tell her?" Karin felt like she was begging.

"Gina?"

"Cynthia. You know I meant Cynthia."

He laughed. He told her he did know. And, yes, sure, he'd tell her. If it came up, he'd tell her. She had as much of a right as anyone to know, after all.

Outside the diner, she smoked the cigarette he offered. She was getting away from herself, and it was kind of nice. She left lipstick on the cigarette like a filthy whore. She blew out smoke like a true, furious dragon at the height of its powers, scaled wings beating wide enough to block the horizon.

She tried to forget about it at school. All of it: her husband, Cynthia, Cynthia's husband, Gina. But it proved difficult. There had been a recent outbreak of tragedies in the school, and those were where her mind was meant to be. But the tragedies—cancer and cancer—seemed frivolous, overly dramatic. It felt—though she knew, of course, it wasn't—like getting bent out of shape about student council elections.

Because it felt a lot like a student campaign. The student council had printed up t-shirts for the girl with leukemia in tenth grade: Go Gail! in pink and yellow. And now there were purple armbands for the boy, a Senior. He had brain cancer. He was dying. No one would make t-shirts for a dying boy. How awkward those shirts would be, rumpled at the bottoms of drawers, to be found and pressed to faces in the spring, or maybe the summer, if the boy were very lucky. (Lucky: this was how he was spoken of in the teacher's lounge, in faculty meetings in the rush for cookies and coffee before the head of school began to drone on about what ought to be done in the event of a school shooting, or a student's cheating. The boy could be—and was, really, already—lucky. He had lived to get into college. He wouldn't have to lose his hair. It wasn't like he was a young child. It wasn't like he was married, or had a young child. All these things.)

So, armbands, which could be easily thrown away.

Of course it was awful. Out loud, it was awful. But it didn't feel quite real. Not nearly as real, certainly, as her life. Her life. How long it had been since she'd felt herself to have one. But here it was, undeniably: she was a spouse being cheated on. And this was awful (Not as awful as cancer!), but it was also sordid. It was *hers*. She would hold on to the facts of it, turn them over and over in her mind until she found the sharpest edge, and she would use that edge to cut off her husband's dick. And he would look at her, dick-less, and with wonder. I didn't know what you could do, he would say.

Karin didn't often go to book launches, but she made an exception for Cynthia's. She was a big supporter of Cynthia's, she explained to Henry.

"Great," he said, looking her right in the eyes, a man with nothing to hide.

His lying embarrassed her. She had underestimated him. It was as if he'd suddenly revealed himself to be—after all this time of clumsiness, of tripping over shoelaces and non-existent cracks in the sidewalk—a trapeze artist.

"It'll be like a date night," Karin said.

"Of course, I'll be working," said Henry. "It's part of the job."

Henry put on his shoes. She'd bought him these shoes as a gift, sort of. He had picked them out. She'd had them wrapped. She paid from their joint checking account.

"Of course," she said.

The book launch took place in Cynthia's parents' house, which was probably better described as an estate. There were actual waiters in bowties passing around platters of hors d'oeuvres that Cynthia kept telling everyone to eat. For her part, Cynthia was carrying around a glass of water, from which she occasionally, delicately, sipped.

She put a bony hand on Karin's shoulder. "I imagine still breastfeeding—the baby is how old?— must make you hungry. Hold out your hand."

Karin didn't know what else to do, so she did. Cynthia placed a miniature quiche in the very center of Karin's palm, closed Karin's fingers around it. "There you go," she said. "There are plenty more. Beauty standards these days are unrealistic."

And then she turned, gliding on to her next victim.

Karin knew she'd just failed some kind of test. But she figured she might as well eat the mini quiche, which was quickly oiling her fingertips. She ate it in one bite and came a little close to choking.

The reading took place in a room Cynthia called "the study." Karin would have called it "my whole goddam apartment." Chairs were arranged in rows, as in a theater, with a podium set up in the center. There were even steps leading up to it.

"I've got to sit next to Cynthia," Henry explained. "Work, you know."

Yes, she told him, she did know. She found Frank and sat next to him. "Where's Gina?" she said.

He laughed, patted her on the top of the head as if to tell her what a good dog she was being. "That's not something let's talk about."

She felt as though the quiche actually had gone down the wrong way, after all, and was now stuck some place it shouldn't have been. "She doesn't know?"

"All right," said Frank. "I think this conversation is done." He stood and moved to the back row.

She felt like crying. Where were all the signs she kept missing? Where were all the betweens she was supposed to be reading? It was so much less evolved, so much more mundane than she'd imagined. Of course Frank would prefer, for as long as possible—and then, even a little longer than that—to pretend. Of course there would never be a conversation with Cynthia in which Gina, if there even was a Gina, would come up.

Cynthia stepped up to the podium. "*Bad Hair*," she began, in a breathy, little girl voice. "I'm going to read from a passage in the middle of the book." She licked the tip of her finger and turned some pages. The dry rustle was the only sound in the room. Henry cracked a knuckle, an awful habit Karin really should talk to him about.

"Karin hated her hair," Cynthia read.

(After the reading, Cynthia would explain, during the hasty Q&A begun by Henry, that Karin of the bad hair was actually a modernized, but creatively veiled Anna Karenina. Karin as in Karenina. It was bullshit, of course, but Karin would find herself impressed with Cynthia's attempt at discretion.)

"Her hair was frizzy and flat." Cynthia stopped, used two fingers to push her too-large glasses higher up on her nose. "This included her pubic hair. She was married to a man who didn't see her."

Cynthia read until the new, better lover was introduced, and then she stopped, bit her lip. Twirled a strand of hair around her finger. She stood very still inside her tent of a baby-doll dress. She stood there until Henry started clapping and everyone else took the cue. Then she kept standing, even after the applause had stopped, long enough for it to pick up again, this time half-heartedly, grudgingly.

And Karin found herself, sort of, almost, understanding why taking care of Cynthia, why fucking Cynthia, might be appealing. How nice to tell someone who really needed to hear it, I like you! You're great! I think you're special!

She didn't confront him—there were the children. There was her new understanding. There was teaching. Or, rather, there was the tenth grade classroom where Karin was at that moment not teaching, because Gail (of "Go Gail!" fame), her terrible wig curled into ringlets, was seated at Karin's desk. A heap of armbands for the cancer boy were spread out in front of her.

"These things really actually matter," Gail explained, gesturing at the armband on her own thin wrist. "They show our support, which in the end does make a difference."

They cost ten dollars apiece, and it was unclear to Karin where, exactly, the money was going. She really hated to think it, but her strong suspicion was that it was being used to fund even more armbands.

The other students made wincing faces to show they

understood and cared.

Sally O'Malley, beloved in the teacher's lounge for her rhyming first and last names and voice like helium, waved a twenty in the air. "Can I have two more?"

Karin froze for a moment. "Two more": she'd heard "tumor."

Her star student, Alex, raised his hand. Even though it seemed Gail had successfully hijacked the class (who could reprimand a recent cancer patient?) Alex had his notebook open already, his highlighter ready, pen in hand, at attention.

"When Ophelia drowns with all her flowers," he said, "maybe she's deflowering herself."

Sally O'Malley nodded thoughtfully. "I like tulips," she said, and then they were all lost to Karin in a stampede of laughter and sex jokes—Tulips: two lips! That open! Sally, hiding her face between her hands, blushed delightedly at her lucky, unintended win. And then the jokes became less inspired, but no less thrilling to her students, devolving into the usual references to cherries and bananas.

Sex! Wasn't it a gas.

Alex stayed after class. "But what do you think of that idea?" he wanted to know.

She loved it, she told him. The idea would make a truly wonderful essay.

He beamed, reminding her of her youngest son, so proud of himself now that he was beginning to walk, belly thrust forward, pattering feet unsteady, his smile dazzling. Karin realized her opportunity had arrived. The classroom had emptied out, and it was just the two of them, Alex skinny and eager, pimpled at the neck like a raw chicken, dandruff dusting his very starched collar. It might be, even, her last chance. She could reach over right now and touch that perfectly starched collar of his shirt.

She could remove his glasses. She could let him have her on the desk. She could get him to rip her shirt open, buttons be damned. (Though there were her potentially-leaking breasts to consider.)

But she wasn't going to fuck her student. She wasn't going to be a filthy whore. It was a terrible thing to realize, that she actually was what everyone took her for: wife, mother, schoolteacher. A vanilla cookie of a person, trustworthy and safe and invisible. Something no one minded, but that no one actually wanted. A woman, betrayed, who wished she had not been.

Guns Are Safer for Children
Than Laundry Detergent

He had a gun. There was a gun in the house. A gun a gun a gun.

Yael told herself to stop it. Boaz was Tamar's husband. Tamar was her sister. Half sister. Anyway, he could have a gun if he wanted a gun.

The gun was resting in some kind of gun holder attached to his belt. "You can hold it," Boaz said. He was cheerful to the point almost of whistling.

"It might be better if I didn't," Yael said. "Who knows what I'd do with a gun."

"Guns are safer for children than laundry detergent," Tamar said.

"I bet," said Yael. "Kids, right?" She had no idea of what she was saying. She just wanted to be agreeable, but the words' meanings were slipping away from her. It was also the way she felt after too many sleeping pills.

"You look beautiful, by the way," Yael said. "I can't believe there was just a baby *inside* you."

"Oh, stop it," Tamar said, but she was smiling.

Yael had come to Dallas (a Jewish community on the rise! Tamar had explained on the phone, sounding disconcertingly middle-aged) for the bris. His ritual circumcision, Yael'd had to translate for her non-Jewish friends. You know how it goes, on the baby's eighth day of being alive, we just put him on a pillow, chop some skin off his penis and chant joyously. Everything normal in Hebrew was terrible in English. Or maybe it was that everything normal in Judaism was terrible.

But Tamar was Yael's favorite of her half-siblings—the others mostly ignored her. When Tamar had called to invite Yael to Dallas for the bris, which coincided so nicely with the Thanksgiving long weekend, all Yael could think of saying was of course. She'd love to. Tamar's son. Yael remembered when she used to babysit for Tamar, idly stuffing graham cracker after graham cracker into her mouth, occasionally doing homework, while Tamar lined up de-frocked baby dolls, their scribbled-on bald heads gleaming. Be good, Tamar used to tell the line of baby dolls. Listen and behave. Now Tamar had a real one. It was only too bad that the real husband she'd found to go with it had to have a gun.

"You'd better hurry it up if you want one of your own," Boaz said.

It took her a second to realize he didn't mean a gun.

"Boaz," Tamar said.

"What?" he said. "We're all friends here."

Yael made herself laugh, a wheezy in and out that sounded like a donkey's dying breath.

"See?" Boaz said. "Yael knows what I mean. So you've got to get on it. You and what's his name, your…friend?"

Her "friend." He just couldn't bring himself to say "boyfriend" or, better yet, "the man you've lived with longer than I've even known my wife." Instead, he had to behave as though the thought of a man and a woman cohabitating was so far from his frame of reference it was simply *unfathomable*.

"His name's Sam," Yael said. "I don't know that he's the marrying type. Not like you, Boaz."

"Well, sometimes in the secular world it takes the men a

little while," Boaz said, vaguely.

"Yael's probably tired from the trip," Tamar said. "I'll show you where you're staying."

The bed in the guestroom had been carefully made, a mint centered on the pillow. On the nightstand, a bottle of water, a thin stack of magazines. The room reminded Yael of Tamar's childhood dresser, where she'd kept her treasures: a package of gum, a box of mints, ponytail holders with glued-on, but falling-off, flower petals. Yael felt almost like crying. Tamar always cared too much. There was no protecting someone who cared as much as Tamar did.

"You made it just like a hotel in here," Yael said.

"Did you see the mint?" Tamar said.

"I love it," Yael said. "The perfect touch."

"Boaz doesn't mean everything he says," Tamar said.

"I know," Yael said.

"He keeps the gun in a safe."

"That's good."

"I don't even know the code. I asked him not to tell me. It's just his thing. People in Dallas all have guns. Our rabbi has a gun. It's no big deal, outside New York."

"I get it," Yael said.

And even though she herself had lived for a time in Wisconsin, where no one she knew had even a water gun, she did get it. Talking to Tamar, she got it. The trouble was when Tamar wasn't there to explain it to her. Then everything went right back to being crazy.

"He feels like he has to protect himself," Tamar said.

What else was Yael supposed to say? Yes, it's a big, bad world out there? It's shoot or be shot? We're all a bunch of savage and sun-damaged rapscallions living in a Western?

"He didn't have to bring up Sam," Tamar said.

"It's no trouble. We can talk about Sam all day, if he wants. I'm a fan of Sam's."

The question that was not addressed: Well, then, where is that terrific Sam?

The answer, such as it was, almost made sense, but only from a distance. Up close, it crumbled, pixilated. He was home. Home alone, just like the movie. Lost in New York.

What Tamar wouldn't understand—what Yael herself didn't really understand—was that Yael didn't want to marry Sam. She'd spent her whole life, basically, wanting to get married, but now that she was with someone who wanted to marry her, have a baby with her, she found she'd changed her mind. She didn't think she wanted to end up alone, but, who knew, maybe she actually did. She was in therapy about this. She was taking sleeping pills about this.

"I'm glad you're here," Tamar said.

And then came the bleating infant cry, a car alarm gathering volume and speed.

Tamar stood up from the bed. "I feel like crying all the time," Tamar said. "Is that funny?"

"Everyone feels that way," Yael said. "Totally normal."

She should know. She counseled women who were not totally normal, women who fantasied about throwing their infants out the window, snapping their fragile necks, pressing down on the soft spots in the back of their skulls, and then actually also did it. Or only tried to, in the best of cases. The funny thing was, to them, she was the therapist.

Boaz knocked on the door. "The baby's crying," he said.

Yael unpacked. She was a terrible packer, and everything was wrinkled, even the stuff she'd thought she folded well. She hung up the long-sleeved, below knee-length, collar bone-covering dress she wore to any and all Orthodox functions. It occurred to her that her Orthodox family (half family) might think she was a little homeless. Destitute, at least. What was wrong with them? Shouldn't her step-mother pull her father aside and tell him it looked like Yael might be in need of some help, wink-wink?

She ate Tamar's mint.

She stretched out like a starfish on the bed, wiggling her toes over the covers, jazzing her hands. The bed was just a twin, but still, there was so much space. She felt like she could wrap herself in cashmere lengths of space.

She'd promised Sam she'd call, so she called Sam.

"Put Wendy June on the horn," she said. Wendy June was their imaginary child, their trial run, their what our life would look like if.

Most women on the wrong side of forty weren't content with imaginary children. They had real children. Or they wanted real children. What wasn't to want? Who didn't want love, right? Or, if they didn't want children, they knew this, too. They liked their lives just as they were, thank you very much. They traveled. Indecision, Yael knew, was an ugly color on a woman whose pregnancy, if it even happened, would be categorized as geriatric.

But Sam understood, or said he understood. He told her he was fine with waiting. As though waiting, if the waiting went on long enough, were not itself a choice.

"Wendy June can't come to the phone," he said. "She's being punished. I have her in timeout."

"That Wendy June. What'd she do this time?"

"She refused to come to the dinner table. She's thankful for nothing, she said."

"Not even turkey?"

"Not even yams."

"She's acting out," Yael said. "Probably misses her mom."

"Still, that's no excuse. She's supposed to start first grade soon, you know."

"There's a strict no-nut policy at the school," Yael said. "So we'll have to be careful when we buy her snacks. And we have to remember school supplies. Did you get the list from her new teacher?"

"Already on the refrigerator," Sam said. "Glue sticks, markers and scissors. I can't believe we're paying 20,000 a year for her to do art projects. Isn't first grade supposed to be serious?"

"Everyone's all about the coddling these days. But our Wendy June deserves the best, don't you think?"

"I only wish she weren't so spoiled," Sam said.

"I know it," Yael said. "We've got to start doing a better job. She's not a baby anymore. Six years old is a big girl."

"Time really flies," Sam said.

Only a few weeks ago, Wendy June had been an infant. But an imaginary infant was like having an imaginary housefly. There wasn't much to work with. So time had zipped ahead, and here they were, the proud parents of an almost-first-grader.

"She has a uniform this year. And the lice check. So you might want to get that taken care of before I get back."

"How's Wendy June's new cousin?"

"Half cousin. He reminds me of Wendy June when she was born. It feels like only weeks ago."

"Time really flies," Sam said.

"You said that already."

"What?"

"You already used that line."

Just like that, the conversation was broken. It was like coming up for air in a pool. It turned out you weren't a mermaid at all. You were just a person. You needed to breathe.

"Boaz has a gun, you know," Yael said.

"What do you mean, 'you know'? How am I supposed to know?"

"It's a way of talking," Yael said. "Not everything is an accusation."

Sam had wanted to come with her. He was fine with sleeping in separate rooms, even, as Tamar and Boaz would have surely insisted. I'm your boyfriend, he'd said. And she hadn't meant to, but she made a heart with her two hands and said, My boyyyyfriend. It was really almost an accident, that heart. She might've meant to do something else with her hands. She didn't really mean to thump the hands-heart against her real heart and say, Va-va-voooom!

"Anyway," Yael said now. "Tamar said guns are safer for children than laundry detergent. Does that sound like something you've heard?"

"When are you coming back?"

She hadn't given him the exact dates—she didn't know, she'd explained, at which point the visit would become intolerable.

"I'll be back to put Wendy June on the bus for her first day of school."

"Yael."

"Sa-am."

She liked to give his names two syllables. When they first met, he'd kept mispronouncing her name and she could never figure out a good way to get back at him. How do you pronounce that again? she'd say. Bam, is it?

"Just tell me when you'll be back."

"I'll stay until the mohel's had his way with the little guy."

Sometimes, it was as soon as she said something that she heard how wrong it was.

"I'll bring you a bagel and shmear. And blue and white jelly beans, if they have any."

"Blue and white for Israel?"

"Blue and white for boys."

"It's getting late," Sam said.

"Give Wendy June a kiss for me," Yael said. "Tell Wendy June she's loved."

Yael swallowed the sleeping pill without water, one straight line down. She went right to bed. Closed her eyes. Waited. The psychiatrist had instructed Yael to go to sleep immediately after taking the sleeping pill. Stay up after taking a pill and you ran the risk of night-eating, night-shopping, night-cracking-the-code-to-the-safe-and-shooting-your-brother-in-law-through-the-head. Half brother-in-law.

The psychiatrist had also told her to only take the pills in case of an emergency. Yael didn't want to wind up addicted, the psychiatrist said. No, she didn't want that. But she did want to sleep. Was it possible that every night was an emergency?

Yael thought she wouldn't fall asleep, that this would be the night the pills stopped working for her. She thought this every night, which, according to the psychiatrist, was part of Yael's problem. Then she found herself in a dream. In her dream—which she knew and didn't know was a dream—she was one of her patients, Courtney, a young mother who couldn't stop talking about how much she wanted to drown her child in the bathtub. Courtney had checked herself into the hospital before she could do anything. She spent her sessions begging Yael please not to send her home. I don't know what I'll do, Courtney said. Please, I don't know what I'll do. In real life, Courtney's child was a three-month-old named Jack, but in the dream, the child was Wendy June, age six.

In the dream, Yael was Courtney, but she was also herself. She was also herself, but she looked like Boaz. She was holding a gun. Take it, she said to Courtney. Hold it. Feel how heavy it is. Does it feel heavy to you? Wendy June, who was there and not there, began to cry. She had lopsided pigtails, scabs cross-hatching her knees. She was wearing glasses with pink plastic frames that hooked around the ears.

It was the baby who was crying. Yael was awake, and sweating.

"I hope he didn't wake you," Tamar said when Yael staggered into the kitchen for coffee. It was 10:30. Yael was a despicable cretin of a person, a leech on society. Waking up at 10:30 was fine only if you were a teenager and your body was using the time to unfurl and lengthen, turn into itself.

"I was up," she said. "Just catching up on some paperwork in my room."

"You always work too hard," Tamar said.

A laugh and a half. She'd discharged Courtney that Wednesday, just in time for Thanksgiving; she'd had to, because Courtney's insurance had run out. But Yael might have spent longer on the phone with Courtney's insurance representative. She might have written a letter—to whom? Maybe called a lawyer. Gone to Courtney's house, broken down the front door, and gotten baby Jack out of there herself. Instead, You'll be fine, she'd told Courtney. You're a good mother. Nothing will happen.

"I can hold the baby, if you want," Yael said.

The problem with holding the baby was how aware Yael was of the softness of his skull, the weakness of his neck. He only weighed seven pounds, a scattering of ounces. Here was an entire person. She only had to open her arms, and that would be it for him. How many important things had she dropped in her life?

She smelled his head. There was nothing, she told Tamar, better than smelling a baby's head.

The bris, scheduled for first thing in the morning, was packed with people Yael didn't know, and also her family. Yael's father, smelling as he always did, of cloves, gave her a hug. Tamar should have babies more often, if that was going to be what it took to see her! Her stepmother, in her for-special-occasions wig, told Yael she was so happy to see her. It was so nice of Yael to be there. As though Yael were not part of the family, but a guest who was welcome enough.

The women's section in the sanctuary was separated from the men's by a thick curtain no one could see through. The reason for this, Yael had learned as a child, back when she was a Yeshiva girl, was women were too attractive to men. Men couldn't focus on God when there were women afoot. So they had to be separate. In some shuls, the women's section was a balcony looking down into the men's, because women, Yael had been taught, were closer to God and would never be tempted to ignore Him. Also, women didn't get attracted to men. Attraction was just a man thing.

So Yael could hear but not see the men as they crowded around the baby, who had been carried in on a white pillow edged in lace.

The rabbi began reciting the blessings, and then the terrible cry rose up. Yael was glad she couldn't see the sharp-tipped knife going in, the spurting, she imagined, of blood. She pictured a battlefield.

Tamar was holding her mother's hand, crying without sound. The tears were effortless. They just came down.

Boaz echoed the rabbi's prayer, and the men in congregation responded to his call, their voices rising up together. The baby's name at first sounded to Yael like part of the prayer, and she missed it, but she wasn't the only one. Women around her whispered—what was it? Did you hear?

"It's Shalom Yedidyah," Tamar whispered to Yael. Her shoulders were straight now; she was wiping away the leftover tears. Shalom, which meant peace. Yedidyah had been their grandfather's name.

The food part of the bris was in the shul's basement, referred to, optimistically, as the "party room." The decorations, though, were lovely. Bouquets of It's A Boy! balloons were tethered to the floor, just barely, with clusters of silver bells; at the center of each table, there were the fake lace satchels of blue and white jelly beans Yael had hoped for. Everyone shoved past each other in a flurry of elbows and indignant excuse mes (from the very polite). There were vats of scrambled eggs assembled from a powder, piles of syrup-sticky French toast, bagels with the everythings somehow already scarce—at any time, it could all run out.

Yael was glad Sam hadn't come. Sam never knew how to manage himself at these kinds of functions. He refused to push. He believed in waiting his turn. And he had all kinds of theories about why Orthodox Jews were rude; it was inherited trauma, he'd explained to Yael, more than once. She didn't even know what that was supposed to mean. All she knew was how much she hated it when he started to talk like that—like he knew what it was to be a Jew, or her. At least he cared about something real, he told her. At some point, someone had to care about something real. That fight was an old standby of theirs, a classic rerun you could catch any time.

Boaz stood up, clinked his glass, said thank you to everyone, mazel tov to everyone. Joy belonged to everyone. "We named him Shalom," he said, "because we have a great hope for him." Boaz continued on to say how troubled these times were, how scary it was to be in the world, a Jew in the world. There were wars that wouldn't let up; there were bombings, people afraid to leave their homes, but leaving their homes anyway.

"We hope the world will be different for him," Boaz said. He looked so small and thin up there, his belt looped and tightly buckled. Stripped of his gun.

Everyone was silent for a slip of a second, and then came the Amens, the tipping back of glasses, the resumed scramble for food.

A woman holding the hand of her daughter, a pig-tailed Wendy June doppelganger, wedged herself into a non-space beside Yael. "Can you just help me grab..." she said, but Yael ignored her, was already reaching over her. There was one everything bagel left, and it was going to be hers. An Orthodox function was the only place anymore that felt like home.

And then she went home to Sam. It was late afternoon when she got back to the apartment, shading already into evening. Dinnertime, homework-time, for people who had kids.

"Honey, I'm ho-ome," she said, flinging her arms into a ta-da!

He didn't answer, and it struck Yael—of course. Of course he was gone. He'd put up with her long enough. Enough was enough. He'd left her. He'd left her without even ever marrying her. All she could do to note the decimation of their relationship, of almost six years of her life—and the almost six that really counted—was change her status on Facebook.

Here it was, the end of the world, and it looked like this: a woman with a small suitcase in an empty apartment.

The toilet flushed. "Yael?" he said.

Of course he hadn't left. He was right here, of course.

She noted that his hands, as he left the bathroom, were bone-dry. If not for her, there probably wouldn't even be soap in the bathroom.

"My flight got in on time," she said.

"Glad to hear it," he said.

"I got you those jellybeans," Yael said. "The blue and whites? You should have seen how many of those there were."

He didn't say anything. He didn't have to say anything. Because: How could he have seen how many there were? He hadn't been invited. She hadn't invited him.

He smiled into his fist.

She moved to the bedroom to unpack her sad little suitcase, the awful dress Sam liked to call her "Jew dress." Or used to like to call her Jew dress.

He followed her in. So that was his move, then. To watch her unpack, but not help her unpack.

He sat on the bed, totally dressed, even with his shoes still on, watching her.

She matched a pair of socks, one shorter than the other.

"Maybe we should think about aging Wendy June on up," she said. "First grade is a drag. All we have to look forward to is missing teeth. Sixth grade, I think, is when it gets interesting. Because then it's puberty, and you can bet our Wendy June's hair is going to frizz."

Yael drew her hands together and then gigantically apart. "*Pffff.* It's going to be *cotton candy.* And she'll get her period. We'll have to make sure she knows in advance that she's not dying. And that those little pieces in it are perfectly normal. You know I used to think they were teeny-tiny globules of baby skin? Even though definitely I knew about sex—the period was post-Orthodox. But I thought maybe sperm could come up from the drains and get me in the bath. So I was always super relieved, and super guilty. Dead babies every month."

He just looked at her. It was like being with a mute. It was like bowling with bumpers. It was like punching someone who wouldn't punch back.

"Or we could put her in high school. She can have her first kiss in high school, and you can tell her boyfriend that you'll knock his lights out if he even so much as lifts a finger to your baby girl. If he even so much as ruffles a hair on her head. We'll catch her smoking pot and ground her for weeks. And then we'll smoke the pot, and she'll find us, and we'll all have a good belly laugh about that.

"Let's send her to college. We deserve an empty nest, don't you think, after all we've been through with our Wendy June? She can do a liberal arts degree and we can support her forever."

Yael guessed it was possible that she'd go on speaking forever. Maybe this would be their life now. She'd just talk and talk and talk and eventually she'd be her mother.

"Should we just go ahead and have a child?" she said.

Right away: "You'd want a child?"

She hadn't actually thought he'd answer. She'd thought she knew his hand, but he'd tricked her. When had they last had this conversation? Not since the earliest incarnation of the relationship, when they were trying each other on for size, back when she was doodling ironic hearts around his name, writing hers as Mrs. Yael Murphy. They'd had this conversation then, but back then they'd been laughing. A little you or me, could you just picture it?

"We won't name her Wendy June," Sam said. He was speaking more quickly now. "Or him. It. We'll give it a real name."

She didn't say anything. Everything she had was wrinkled. Everything smelled. She'd only been gone a few days, but the clothing barely looked like anything she'd ever look twice at, let alone own.

"Oh," he said. "You were just *saying*."

"I wasn't just saying," she said.

What she wanted to say—Wendy June is enough. Not the time warp Wendy June she'd summoned just now, and who lingered still, like the sound of a slap. The Wendy June they'd made up together. The Wendy June who had been an infant, but now was in first grade, and had to get her hair checked for lice. Their Wendy June, who, come Thanksgiving, hadn't even been thankful for yams. They'd never do better than her. Wendy June was so much.

FUN DAY

Every year, there is one day when everyone loves the three sisters. Never mind the oldest's going to therapy right next door to the school bus-stop, or the youngest's penchant for feeding her lunch to stray animals every day (sometimes to a cat, sometimes to a dog), which must by now surely have translated into rabies. Or the overall oddness of the middle sister, who twists her thin arms strangely when she doesn't know the answer to a question, and who has too many rows of pencils, all lined up exactly on her desk, point to point.

This day is Fun Day.

Their father, William, is CEO of a company (that sells pants? belts?), and Fun Day is like office picnics they have seen on TV—the way real farms are like the ones for ants. It makes them gloat. There is cotton candy, there are games wherein stuffed animals can be won, and there are sideshows.

The oldest, Elizabeth, and the middle, Lucille, decide to try their luck at a game. "Try their luck" is a phrase belonging to their father. They know they will win. They always win on Fun Day. They can fail to squirt water into the clown's mouth every time—every time! what are the odds of that?—and still, the man behind the counter will say, We have a winner! They are the daughters of the CEO, and so, on Fun Day, as they are not on any other day, they are royalty.

Elizabeth has her eyes set on a giant bear that will not, of course, prove soft—these kinds of bears, she knows from experience, are always stuffed with what feels like newspaper. Lucille would like the enormous frog. There will be no need to fight. After they lose wildly, each will get the prize of her choosing, the screaming of other children rising up delightfully around them.

But Sophie, who is the youngest, decides she would like to visit the sideshow. She visits the fortune-teller, because she wants to know the future. This is their last Fun Day, their mother, Anna, says, because it's true: she's dying. The chemo is a troop of good soldiers attacking the bad cancer, the doctor has said. The idea of soldiers marching through her mother's body, attacking cells who are not soldiers, and who cannot fight back, horrifies Sophie. She likes better to think of it as medicine, a kind of viscous, cherry-flavored sludge.

Sophie is curious to find out when, exactly, her mother will die. She would like to be prepared, with a face most right for mourning, which she practices at home in the bathroom mirror. The face is devastated, but dignified. She will hold her chin high and lower her eyes, so the eyelashes almost touch her cheekbones. She will bite, just lightly, her lower lip. Oh, the mourners will say. What a trooper. And the sleeves of her black dress will be just a bit too long, a reminder to all that she is now a daughter without a mother.

The fortuneteller is stationed inside a tent that smells like lavender. There are curtains made of beads Sophie must part in order to get to her. The fortuneteller has no visitors, so, she tells Sophie, she may sit down right away. Sophie holds out her hand to shake, because she is practicing already the kind of motherless daughter she will be, which is a polite one. But the fortuneteller simply looks at Sophie's hand, as though she has never seen one before.

"I'm Sophie," says Sophie. She lines up her heels so it's like she's a dancer while she waits.

"Oh!" The fortuneteller sounds just like Sophie's mother already out the door and just remembering she's forgotten her wig. Her gums show when she smiles. "You can call me Madame Felicia."

"Do you have cards?" Sophie says. "Because I'm looking to find out about death."

Madame Felicia nods. She takes out a pack of cards and flips over four. She sets them down on her table one at a time. There is a willow tree with all its branches weeping, a sky colored in with sunset, an alligator sliding on a lily pad, also a two of spades Madame Felicia tells Sophie to never mind.

Madame Felicia taps her fingernails on all the cards before stopping at the alligator. "There's your death," she says. "Are you headed to Florida? You've got to watch out over there. You wouldn't believe the racket; they're in the toilets."

Sophie bites the inside of her cheek. "Not really."

"It'll probably just be the chemotherapy that does it, anyway," Sophie offers. Madame Felicia blinks.

"You're supposed to cost money, but I get you for free," Sophie says, and she flashes the card that says, yup, she's her father's daughter.

She leaves the tent so quickly, she imagines she's a blur. The curtain of beads is already waving closed behind her when Madame Felicia calls out, "Wait!"

Sophie does wait. Elizabeth wouldn't, but Sophie does.

"We forgot about your palms," Madame Felicia says.

Sophie returns to the table and holds out her palms like a baffled cartoon character.

Madame Felicia's fingernails feel like one of Lucille's pencils as they travel inside Sophie's palms. "You have a nice, long lifeline," she says. She drags a nail down the center of Sophie's palm. "See?"

She sounds the way mothers do on TV: There, there.

Sophie finds Lucille and Elizabeth eating cloudy cones of cotton candy.

"The duchess is back," says Elizabeth. Because Sophie is the youngest, she, like any doll, belongs to Elizabeth. Elizabeth's full name for Sophie is The Duchess of Adorability, sometimes Duchee (pronounced Du-she) for a nickname. "Duchess, would you like some cotton candy? Do duchesses eat cotton candy?"

"Duchesses eat corndogs," Sophie says.

"Corndogs are bad for braces," says Lucille, who has braces. "With the cotton candy, it melts."

They flash their cards, and it's corndogs for everyone, including Lucille, who often changes her mind. She's right about the braces.

They arrive at the Fun Day picnic sticky with sugar and salt and sweat. Their parents are on a blanket with one plate of watermelon and a second for the spit-out pits, slick as beetles. Their mother waves them over.

"Girls," she says, because it's easier to lump them; the three names are always one too many. "Over here."

William, who does not often speak, glances up at the sun. One time, though, soon after Anna was diagnosed, he'd walked into the living room where they were watching a show about a woman who ran into her husband, even though he was dead. The reason she was able to run into him was his face had been transplanted onto a man who had no face. William stood in front of the set, as though he didn't understand about television.

"I know where to buy maxi-pads," he'd said.

"Are you girls having fun at Fun Day?" Anna asks now.

"There's an alligator in my future," Sophie says.

"There's a frog in my present," says Lucille, lifting the stuffed frog she's been dragging around. There are bits of grass and dirt wading up to the frog's anatomically impossible belly button, implied by an unraveling string.

Anna offers William a Percocet, and when he declines, she shrugs, tossing it into her mouth with élan, no water necessary. The Percocet is not new, but when she takes them now, people's eyes cloud and their foreheads crinkle, fans abruptly closed. She is so brave.

Nothing has worked out the way she and William had imagined: their dream of a boy and a girl immediately disrupted by the emergence of Lucille, and even the compromise going bust, with Sophie. So, then the reluctant revision: three girls, who would dress alike and wear bows in their hair. Elizabeth had been the one to ruin it, pulling out her hair in clumps, and then of course came the therapy, even though no one went to therapy, and the cabinets filled more quickly than one might have imagined with tranquilizers. Even the dog didn't work out, leaving droppings in carefully chosen corners, perpetually humping any available leg. His name was Pierre, in homage to the France where they would go to retire, cheerful and plump and not yet too old. Where they were to have gone.

Lucille's voice, made silky by the Percocet, has been threading all the while through Anna's thoughts, and it is surprising to realize Lucille is still speaking about the carnival games.

"We won a lot," Lucille is saying.

"We got a lot of prizes, she means," Elizabeth corrects. "We were never even runner-ups."

"Maybe next Fun Day," Anna says, and throws back her head, and laughs.

They return to the hotel, which is very fancy, William wants them to know. He has said this already four times. They are meant to rest up for a while so they'll be fresh for the fireworks. There is baby grand in the lobby, and Anna sits down on the bench. She and Elizabeth both know how to play the piano, though Elizabeth is, terribly, now better at it. Together, they play songs of Anna's choosing: "The Sun Will Come out Tomorrow"; "I'm Still Here"; "Being Alive"; "I Whistle a Happy Tune." Anna enjoys the inappropriateness of the songs. The sun sure *will* come out, I'll *certainly* still be here, a funny, *wonderful* business isn't it, being alive. And here I am, whistling a happy tune. Whoot whoot whoot.

It's a loop she says she would like to have playing at the funeral.

It's a loop she would like for Elizabeth to play. The other girls can't play and are on their own to figure something out. Maybe Lucille, at least, will draw some kind of picture, make use of that odd pencil collection.

It's harder than it used to be for Anna to play; among the chemo's many side effects—side effects! as though the effects were incidental!—is a numbness to the hands. But she actually will, she'll go to her grave playing the piano. Surely, one pie-faced social worker at the hospital had said, Elizabeth's playing is a solace. Isn't it wonderful, how Anna will live on through her daughter? It will be, according to the social worker, like Anna's spirit is speaking with Elizabeth every time she plays. "How about that?" she'd said to Anna. "Mom can keep on speaking," as though Anna were a mother to her own self.

There are getting to be more and more such social workers, each pouncing, in her own way, on Anna's daughters. The social workers collectively believe the girls are exhibiting signs of grief, which, in this *situation* is perfectly natural. (It's like a game everyone is playing, this avoiding of the word "cancer." It's like that stupid board game Lucille and Sophie love.) Well, the girls were peculiar before any of this happened.

Of course, this isn't the kind of thing you say out loud, if you're dying. The dying are supposed to selfless and graceful as young nuns kneeling in prayer, gifting all who come to sit solemn vigils at their bedsides with a wise and far-reaching benevolence, and benediction. It isn't that she doesn't love the girls. It isn't a question of *love*.

But the social workers think, no, the girls are fantastic, with only one perfectly natural, and solvable problem. And the social workers hand out pamphlets and warm smiles like perfume samples. The pamphlets come with advice like, There is no one way to grieve, and, It is perfectly normal to feel angry, and, It is okay to feel sad, and also, Sometimes punching a pillow can help. Very, very much. The smiles come with odors of cheap chocolate or butterscotch sucking candy. The social workers are the last people on earth Anna would call upon if she were dying— though, whoops! she already is. She will not live on through Elizabeth's playing. Anna will play with her now, and once she is dead, she'll be dead. Her "spirit" will not emerge and retreat, stubborn and annoying as a cuckoo from a clock.

As she plays, Anna's fingers, sluggish as tired children, veer inward, creating the impression of oven mitts. "Are you sure I'm on the right key?" she asks Elizabeth, though they both know she is, of course, not even close. "You're perfect," says Elizabeth, because she and all the rest only lie and lie, and now, as Anna stops playing, not half-way through the song, they all stand up, clapping, calling out, Encore!

At night, all of them say gosh how nice the fireworks look up there in the sky.

The day after Fun Day is like the morning after a dream: startlingly regular. Sophie has been exiled from the hotel room; Elizabeth, claiming to be playing house, has named herself the mother, Lucille the father, and Sophie the teenager daughter. So go on a date, Sophie has been instructed. The castles have been deflated; the Ferris wheel is on its side. Some of the vendors have already disappeared, and the ones left have gates to cover their prizes. There seem to be more mosquitoes in the air, now that there is so much extra room.

Sophie sits on the lawn where the fireworks used to be. There are some stray light-up bracelets and necklaces for which Sophie's family had not needed, as everyone else had, to pay. But now, that that they are the daughters of the CEO means nothing. Fun Day, their last, is over.

Sophie splits a blade of grass right down its center. The smell is earthy and sweet. They've already visited Anna's plot, and there is grass like this in the cemetery, on which Sophie will maybe sit, and weep with gentle dews of tears. The epitaph is all set to read "Devoted wife and mother." Many other tombstones have the same or a similar inscription. This is why William has picked it: he likes to get things right. Anna had wanted: "I may not be composing, but I sure am decomposing!"

This idea, William had told the funeral director, was one caused by the cancer's spreading from breast to bone, and, finally, to brain. But Anna is the same as she's ever been, and the doctor has not mentioned anything about brains at all, except for the one time he tapped his own head and said, "Kishkas" as a modest declaration of the superior inner workings of his own brain. What he'd gotten right that time was the root of Anna's fickle memory; it was the chemotherapy at work, that army. And how he must have gone through that day congratulating himself: Boy, if he didn't have a terrific bedside manner!

Sophie is now on the grass, closing her eyes but still seeing the muted kaleidoscope of sun beneath her eyelids. Without this, here's death: stiff as a board. But her mother will not be also light as a feather; corpses are said to be heavy. And now Sophie feels a presence, a hovering body above her. So here she is, feeling and seeing and not dead.

She opens her eyes, and there is Madame Felicia, but without the flowing dress and rippling necklaces, the bracelets extending up to her elbows, the knuckle-hugging rings. She looks like a person Sophie might pass on the street or see from a moving car. She is younger than Sophie'd realized, and, without the flowing dress, without the table between them, she sees Madame Felicia's just pregnant enough not to be someone about whom Sophie's mother would say, Well, she's really gone and let herself go.

Madame Felicia sits down next to Sophie, but Sophie doesn't sit up. She stays lying down. "I was hoping I'd catch you," says Madame Felicia. "Just after you left, I had a thought about your card."

"I was getting corndogs," Sophie says. "I get them free."

"I realized I read the card backward. The alligator actually means the opposite of death. So, life."

Sophie narrows her eyes. What Madame Felicia's saying is what her mother would call "a leap." This is what she'd said when Sophie and her sisters all chipped in to buy her a mug that said, every word in a different color, Number One Mother!"

"That doesn't make any sense," Sophie says. "There aren't any alligators. We're not *going* to Florida."

Madame Felicia rubs her elbow. The skin there, Sophie sees, is wrinkled and dry. "Who's getting the chemotherapy?" Madame Felicia says.

Sophie doesn't really want to think about it, but she can see the beginning of Madame Felicia's breasts from where she is lying down. They are smushed together for being so big. Inside her bra must be silver dollar areolas, sprouting coarse black hairs around the rims, the breasts themselves streaked with veins, drooping, shriveled udders. This is how Sophie's mother's breasts looked, when she had breasts.

Sophie stands up. "Is your husband a fortuneteller, too?"

"I don't have a husband," Madame Felicia says.

"So it'll be just you and the baby. You should put the baby up for adoption."

Madame Felicia puts her hand on her stomach. The way she touches her stomach is as if it's a bedpan—a clean one, but still—she's been asked just a second to hold, and no one's remembered to tell her where or when to put it down.

"Sometimes people don't like it when they're adopted."

"Leave it on a church doorstep. A nun will find it. Nuns can't even have babies, did you know that?"

Now Madame Felicia laughs. "Believe me on this—you wouldn't want a nun for a mother."

If Sophie's mother were a nun, Sophie would be her only child. She would have been rescued from a doorstep where she'd been an abandoned orphan left to die. She would have been almost frozen to death, and when the nuns found her, they would have at first thought she was dead, but then they'd be wrong. And her mother would be married to God.

But Sophie's real mother hates nuns. "Get the hell out of here," she said once to a nun who'd walked so quietly into the room, on shoes softer even than a nurse's. Sophie's mother said she'd be damned if she was going to pray. "Oh no," said the nun. "Prayer is the way to salvation." "Get the hell out," her mother said. "Get her the hell out." There was a bag of her mother's pee that was so yellow it was almost brown, and when her mother yelled, she shook the bed and she shook the bag of pee.

"Your fortunes don't even make any sense," Sophie tells Madame Felicia. "Your baby is going to starve to death."

"Well, do you have some money and an address?" Madame Felicia waits in a way that makes Sophie know she's meant to laugh, but at something that's not funny.

"Money and an address for what?"

"For what?" Sophie says again, because she's all out of patience. She makes it so when she sighs there's no breath left. "I'm a teenager out on a date, but the date is stupid, and now I'm going to go home."

Madame Felicia just sits there, pregnant.

All across Sophie's nose it's like sunburn.

At the funeral, Elizabeth plays "The Party's Over" because she thinks the idea of life with her mother being a party will please and comfort the mourners, and maybe make some of them jealous. She is pretty wrong. So she stops that and begins the loop her mother had requested and the mourners look to her, at each other, and then the floor. They imagine they knew her mother.

The casket is sitting right there.

People pass by it as though it's a couch on sale for the cost of nothing, savaged by moths. An aunt of some sort is holding tissues, an entire box. The funeral officiator stands. He is neither rabbi nor priest, and anyway, it doesn't matter: He has confided that he switches suits to match the occasion. He says Anna lived a life too short, but that she was wonderful and devoted, a consummate mother and wife, maybe gone, but never forgotten. His speech is a song perfectly learned and executed, and he's like a movie star up there: pausing, knitting his lips, ever so slightly bowing his head.

He even has a specific story to recount, chosen like a specialty chocolate from a box colored gold. He has never met Anna. But he knows everything wonderful about her because he interviewed the four of them, asking questions that could only be answered the right way.

He smiles sadly, a gentle shrug of the mouth. His eye contact is impossibly inclusive. He clears his throat and begins. He picks the one about Pierre to tell. (And here there is just a bit of laughter. How about that! A story about a dog at a funeral!)

"The mischief-maker had gotten himself into some prescription medication and ended up needing to be rushed to the animal ER," the officiator says. "For the evening Pierre spent at the hospital, the girls were understandably beside themselves. And Anna went right to her piano, gathering the girls to her side. She played 'Not While I'm Around.'" (And here, the worry arises that he will sing, but no, he knows better.) He says the first line of lyrics like a sentence: "Nothing's going to harm you, not while I'm around."

He looks exactly at everyone. "Anna may no longer be with us, but her gifts will continue to serve and to guide her family, and in this way she is not so far from this world as we might imagine."

The mother he describes is one who makes Sophie jealous, though the mother from the story belongs—belonged—to her. And everything the officiator said is absolutely true; they all sang around the piano, and laughed, and Sophie had even believed, almost, that her mother was right, and could keep Pierre safe, and then she actually had. But he skipped over the part about how Pierre got into the pills: Her mother had been fighting with her father, who'd told her she was the craziest woman he'd ever known, and she rushed to the medicine cabinet and threw a bottle of pills into the air. "I'll show you crazy," she'd said.

The officiator nods now to the mourners, as though he is one of them: deeply, deeply sad. He stands aside to make room for Lucille, whose turn is next. She is a stringy puppet on the podium, smiling like rubber bands are pulling back her lips. Puffs of mosquito bites dot her legs. She's so skinny, Anna used to pretend to fold her, like a shirt.

Lucille delivers a poem that rhymes: "You are the first person I met/ you bet./ You always made good cake/which I did help bake./ You had cancer of the breast/which is not the best."

Sophie trades places with Lucille. She imagines she's the officiator, and this is her job, and she is very fantastic at it. She clears her throat. She almost does a curtsey, but stops herself in time. It's hard to remember, exactly, where it is they actually are. It feels easy to confuse it with the party that comes after a recital. She stands very still. She looks out at the pews, half-filled with aunts and uncles and grandparents and some friends who are her mother's former lovers, but now her former accompanists from when her mother used to play the piano, from when she was so much better than Elizabeth. Sophie is still saying nothing. She is on stage, and here are all these people, watching her. They are here to see her. Imagine: It is her at a piano. She is making the music everyone is listening to. The man accompanying her is someone she might have married. She has been so many different people.

An aunt hisses for Sophie to sit down, honey.

She is herself again.

"Oh, Duchee," Elizabeth whispers once Sophie is back, having eulogized her mother not at all. "No one has a right to be so cute."

Lucille's cheek is hot as fever against Sophie's. Someone new is speaking, not their silent father, whose shoulders make him look small, and whose arms dangle at his sides. There are some tears, handkerchiefs like a sudden flock of doves. Their shoes make shadows on the floor, and all the feet look alone.

Acknowledgments

I would like to thank my wonderful teachers, without whom this book would surely not exist. Thank you to Arthur Budick (1949-2011), who taught me how to read so beautifully and first showed me how I might go about making a life for myself in literature. Thank you to Marisa Schwartz, my first creative writing teacher, who helped me see that I might have something worth saying, in a way worth saying. And to my teachers at the Sarah Lawrence College MFA program: Victoria Redel, Mary La Chapelle, Josh Henkin, Nelly Reifler. Thank you, too, to the teachers whose classes I took outside of academia, at the Sackett Street Writers Workshop and Catapult: Aria Beth Sloss, Nick Dybek, Caroline Zancan, Alex Mar, and Fatima Farheen Mirza. Thank you for treating my writing with such respect and care. And, of course, a gargantuan thank you to Josh Gaylord, who has been my teacher, colleague, mentor, reader, and—after I finally got a view of those clay feet—very good friend.

Thank you to The Wisconsin Institute of Creative Writing for giving me the time and space to work on this collection. Thank you to all the journals who took a chance on individual stories in the collection and first made me believe there could be readers for my work: *The Black Warrior Review, StoryQuarterly, West Branch Wired, Cream City Review, The Florida Review, DIAGRAM, Carve Magazine, Cimarron Review, The Collagist, Bennington Review, Joyland, Image,* and *Witness.*

Thank you to Julia Kenny, who plucked my collection from the slush pile and helped me find its narrative shape—and for all the cheerleading and therapizing along the way. An enormous thank you to Robert Lasner, for bringing this book into the world.

Thank you to my parents, for their endless support. And, too, for the terrific material. Thank you to my siblings, the sole survivors of our childhood. To my nieces and nephews: I'm so thrilled you exist. The eight of you have filled my life with so much more joy than I could ever have imagined possible. Maybe one day your parents will consider you old enough to read this book.